The Community of Lightbearers

·······

Seven Stories of Reclaiming
Wonder and Delight

LORRAINE LUM CALBOW

TURNING
STONE
PRESS

Cover design by Frame25 Productions
Cover art by natalia_maroz c/o Shutterstock.com
Interior design by Howie Severson

Turning Stone Press
8301 Broadway St., Ste. 219
San Antonio, TX 78209
www.turningstonepress.com

Library of Congress Control Number is
available upon request.

ISBN 978-1-61852-106-4

10 9 8 7 6 5 4 3 2 1

Printed in the United States of America

Contents

≈ 1 ≈

Ming Mee: Itchy Feet

The Taoist monk, Li Wu, lives The Way. He listens to the message when he sees the *taiji* symbol—yin and yang, heaven and earth. He knows it is T'ai Yuan, the Buddhist saint, elevated to Goddess of Infinity. He gathers the seeds of a few ancient Dawn Redwood trees. He stops at Dr. Chi Yu's house, a doctor of herbal medicine, who provides a sapling gingko tree. Dr. Yu tells the Taoist monk the ginkgo leaves have repairing powers, and the unusual shape of the gingko leaves will attract the attention of the green warrior. The monk thanks the doctor and proceeds to Yunnan City.

Nestled in the woods near the Dengfend Mountains in the Henan Province, a Shaolin priest, Ma Fun, resides in a monastery with a fifteen-hundred-year-old tradition of studying Chan Buddhism. Ma Fun, well-versed in Wushu and medicine, is invigorating himself with slow movement meditation when the Goddess T'ai Yuan appears to him. She is gazing upon a young boy wearing a garland of colorful leaves that resemble orange duck feet or yellow butterflies or green fans depending of the color of the ginkgo leaves. The boy is cradled in a grove of willow and cassia trees beside a lake. Ma Fun recognizes this ritual site. It is the Xishuangban'na region of the Yunnan Province. Then the priest hears, "Go find him."

His vision spreads among the network of Shaolin priests. An American studying at the monastery offers his Buick. Ma Fun arranges care for the female orphan under his guardianship. When Ma Fun arrives in Yunnan City in the Yunnan Province, possible candidates have been identified. He learns there is a Taoist monk, Li Wu, carrying a sapling gingko tree looking for the boy, too. Remembering his vision, Ma Fun laughs, *What an excellent idea!*

Ma Fun interviews several boys, but they fall short. When he arrives at the home of the boy next on the list, he spots a monk carrying the tiny sapling gingko tree. He wastes no time to introduce himself and explains his mission. The monk and priest hear a child way before they see him. The boy is bargaining. "I promise . . . my brother. . . ." Soon, rising above the wall on the willow tree branch is a young boy with a kind face. His eyes light up when he notices the leaves of the gingko tree. His smile reveals his dimples. He points and asks, "What is that?"

"Hello," respond the two men.

"This is a gingko tree," answers the monk Li Wu. "How old you are?"

"I'm six. In my whole life I've never seen duck feet leaves," shouts the boy.

"Would you like to touch it?" asks Li Wu.

The boy nods yes.

"What is your name?" asks the priest Ma Fun.

"Ming Mee," answers the boy.

"Ming, we have come a long way to find you. May we come in?" asks the Shaolin priest Ma Fun.

The Community of Lightbearers

"I'll ask." The door finally opens and the boy and his father are behind it. The priest and monk explain their mission. The father invites them into the courtyard where the priest Ma Fun spots a familiar structure. The father takes a moment to express gratitude for the efforts made by the Taoist monks and the Shaolin priests to keep the ancient Dawn Redwood trees alive.

The boy's father informs the two men that his son is sensitive to nature. The boy has an affinity toward growing things. The priest Ma Fun and the monk Li Wu are hopeful they have located the right boy, but they still need to confirm it. "Do we have your permission to test the boy?" asks the monk Li Wu.

The father nods in the affirmative.

"Is that a shrine to T'ai Yuan?" inquires the priest Ma Fun.

The boy's father replies, "For many years, our family has relied on the saint T'ai Yuan for guidance. She is the balance of heaven and earth, of female and male, and of right and wrong."

The priest smiles, "It is fitting then that we test the boy by the shrine." The father nods in agreement. Soon the rest of the Mee family arrives: the mother, the grandparents, and the youngest son. They gather around the shrine and the ginkgo tree. The father whispers to Ming, "Do as they ask."

"Wait!" cries the mother. "Our eldest son needs to be here, too." The father returns carrying a frail boy of ten, and he places his son in a bamboo chair near the shrine. Meanwhile, Ming can't contain his fascination with the gingko leaves and inches toward the sapling tree. The monk Li Wu tells Ming, "Go ahead and touch the gingko tree." Ming's small hand reaches out and strokes the leaves, releasing an infectious laugh that fills the court-yard with joy. "What did the tree tell you?" asks the monk Li Wu.

"The tree helps," says the boy. The monk Li Wu gives a smile.

The monk Li Wu pulls out two tiny seeds and pres-ents them to the boy. Ming reaches for the seeds, but the priest Ma Fun stops him. "Ming, T'ai Yuan helps the ancient trees. She is the one who calls the green warriors to assist. Do you understand?"

"Ming," says his father. "Taking the seeds may mean you'll have to leave your family, so answer with care, my son."

"I want the seeds. I don't want to go away," cries the boy. In the end, Ming's curiosity wins out. The strong energy from the seeds draws the boy toward it. He touches the seeds, which explode into massive energy, merging with the medicinal properties of the gingko tree and surrounding Ming and his older brother. The green energy radiates outward, embracing the entire courtyard. Ming sees the energy of the gingko leaves swirling around his older brother. When the green energy subsides, the family screams with delight, as the oldest son is standing firmly on his own two feet.

Tears of joy run down the mother's face as she embraces her son. The father and grandfather beam with relief. The older boy affectionately taps Ming's head and whispers, "I heard your bargain. Thank you."

The Taoist monk and the Shaolin priest know the bittersweet moment to come, so they keep their hearts open. The mother asks, "How long before Ming leaves?" The two agree it would be in a week's time. The priest Ma Fun already has a child under his care. The monk

Li Wu speaks of a doctor and his wife, who are childless, and convinces Ming Mee's parents that being an apprentice to the doctor would be excellent training for a green warrior. Since the doctor and his wife live nearby, Li Wu could easily augment the boy's training.

The priest Ma Fun shares his vision and the initiation for the boy. He knows where the ritual is to take place. He offers to take them there and then to the doctor's home. The Taoist monk Li Wu accepts the offer and expresses his appreciation.

Grandfather surprises his grandson with a gift of a travel bag. "Ming, the Mee family is a family with a long tradition of itchy feet." Grandfather Mee laughs. "We must explore. It's in our blood. I think you are the first green warrior in our family. You will add new secrets to the family." Grandfather Mee touches Ming's heart. "Keep open and magic will happen." He touches Ming's third eye. "Keep open and wonder will appear." Grandfather Mee sighs. "I was free as a bird until your grandmother caught me in her net."

"How did Popo catch you?"

"Popo," laughs Grandfather, "your clever grandmother scratched my feet."

"How come Ba-ba stays in one place?" asks Ming.

"Your father takes after Popo's side, while you take after me."

Ming looks inside the soft carpet-material bag and asks his grandfather, "Gung-gung, perhaps I need another pair of shoes."

"You're right. Why didn't I think of that? No matter . . . this travel bag is for joyful adventures that come from an open heart and mind. Did you know I heard that where you are going there is five-hundred-year-old hermit who lives in the sacred mountains? Wouldn't it be fun to meet him?"

"Gung-gung, if I meet him, I'll get his secrets for a long life and give them to you."

"I'm going to share a secret from my travel bag: A cheerful heart lifts you up and sad heart weighs you down."

"Gung-gung, I'll miss you. I'll miss your stories." Ming sinks into sadness.

"I'll miss you too." With a glint of glee in his eyes, Grandfather Mee says, "But when I think of the stories in your travel bag, I'll be happy. I'll wonder what new things Itchy Feet can be learning today."

Ming's sadness is replaced with excitement when Grandfather Mee magically pulls out another pair of shoes. Ming is in awe and can't figure out how Grandfather did it, but he places the shoes in the bag, for tomorrow a new life begins.

Traveling to the ceremonial site, Ma Fun tells Ming a story. "Dragons are magical and powerful water creatures. When dragons roamed the earth, they kept watch over the water to help stop floods. Each season they made sure the skies opened and poured down so that the trees and plants could live. They lived in underground crystal palaces by the lakes, rivers, and oceans. They carried shiny pearls in their mouths to light their caves. Would you like to visit a special dragon place?"

"Please! Won't Gung-gung be surprised," says Ming.

Ma Fun lets out a jovial laugh and says, "To the Summer Palace of the Mongolian Emperor we go."

At the palace grounds, Ma Fun finds the path and asks the monk Li Wu for the gingko plant for Ming to carry. The path is smooth with weathered granite rocks and a multitude of ferns growing on the ground and on one side of the hill. On the other side are openings between the large rocks. As they travel down the path, they near an opening to a lake, and the air is laden with a sweet and spicy scent. The path opens to a breathtaking view of cassia's grayish bark against the cascading strands of yellow blossom among elongated leaves. The pink blossoms of the cassia trees, willow trees, and mulberry tree give a storybook appearance.

Ma Fun and Li Wu nudge Ming toward the trees. As Ming steps forward, mist envelops him and the trees. The ginkgo leaves form a garland around Ming's head. A limb of a willow tree and a limb of a lone mulberry tree bend together to make a chair for the boy. He sits down, holding tight to the sapling tree. A silkworm from the mulberry tree inches onto the garland of gingko leaves. Slowly the silkworm crawls down the side of Ming's face and proceeds to his arm. "Hold out your arm so I can see you," says the worm.

Ming obeys.

"Hello, I'm Rainbow White. Did you bring that gingko plant for me?" says the worm with a sweet feminine voice, which puts the boy at ease.

"I'm Ming Mee. The plant isn't mine, but I'm sure the Taoist monk Li Wu wouldn't mind giving it to you. You live in a beautiful place."

"The gingko tree will go well in front of my crystal palace. My palace is a wonderful place to hear stories."

"I love stories! Gung-gung and Ba-ba are wonderful storytellers." Thoughts of grandfather, father, and family make Ming sad.

"Look at where you are! Beauty and joy live in the moment and sadness lives in the past," says the worm.

Ming laughs and sadness disappears. "Gung-gung says to be cheerful." A question comes to the boy's mind. He scrunches his eyebrows and asks, "How can a rainbow be white?"

"White is in all colors. I'm a great storyteller too. I think today we should fly across the lake while I tell you a story. Are you ready?"

Ming says, "Yes."

The silkworm vigorously tosses a huge iridescent ball and Ming high into the air, transforms into a dragon, swallows the ball, and scoops Ming onto the soft cushion where the ball had wedged between the fifth and sixth ridges of her back. The dragon asks, "Ming, did you know that the Creator Pangu married T'ai Yuan, the holy woman?"

Ming, who is captivated by the dragon's stag horns, the camel-shaped head, and the snake-like neck, and charmed by the fish scales that shimmer in the sunlight with the colors of the rainbow, doesn't answer.

"Ming, are you awake?"

"I know T'ai Yuan. She protects and guides my family."

"And T'ai Yuan and I are good friends. She is the one who wants me to tell you the story *Journey to the West*. It is a very long story about the Monkey King, Tripitaka who is a monk, and Pigsy, a character who eats too much."

Ming giggles, "I love Monkey King. He steals a magic weapon from the Great Yu, controller of floods. The god can't find the weapon because Monkey King learns how to make it so small that it can't be found. The Monkey King goes to the underworld and changes how long he will live. He goes to the heaven and eats the Immortal peaches that take 6,000 years to ripen. He drinks the Laozi elixir of immortality."

"Yes, children do love the naughty Monkey King, but the Monkey King had to pay for his misdeeds, and he had to accompany Tripitaka from China to India to get the sacred Buddhist scrolls."

"Gung-gung told me to fill my travel bag with adventures and stories."

The dragon dips gently across the lake, but still towers over the trees. "Yes! So my children, will you go on a great journey, too?" asks the dragon.

Ming looks around to see who else the dragon is talking to when he spots a girl with a garland of ginkgo leaves around her head sitting between the seventh and eighth ridges. "Who are you?" he asks. She smiles, turns into a beautiful bird with a head of a golden pheasant, a body of a mandarin duck, a tail of a peacock, a mouth of a parrot, and wings of a swallow with feathers of black, white, red, blue, and yellow, and flies away.

The dragon lands softly on the ground, expels the ball, and changes back into a silkworm lying on Ming's shoulders. "Ming, I want to thank you for the gingko plant and for becoming a green warrior. It's time for me to return to my crystal palace."

"Wait! Aren't you going to tell me how that girl turned into a flying creature or how you can change from a silkworm to a dragon?"

"Ask the holy men who brought you here. Remember, adventures and stories are best enjoyed with an open mind and happy heart." The silkworm disappears and the mist lifts.

Ming runs toward his two companions. Ma Fun plays with the boy by appearing and disappearing among the trees and rocks. Then the boy asks, "What are you doing?"

"This is the move that Monkey King made when he met the Buddhist monk, Tripitaka. Perhaps you would like to play *Journey to the West*?" says Ma Fun to his two companions.

"I'm not playing Pigsy," says Li Wu. "He eats and drinks too much! I'll be the Tripitaka going to India and you two will have to fight it out for who will be the Monkey King and who will be Pigsy."

Ming shouts to Ma Fun, "Wait! Who is the girl? How does a silkworm change into a dragon?"

"Did you meet a dragon? They are good luck," answers Ma Fun.

"Yes, but who is the girl?"

"What did she look like?" asks Ma Fun. Ming describes her and the bird she became. Ma Fun ponders a moment. "What's the dragon's name?"

"Rainbow White," answers Ming.

"Oh . . . one evening I took a little girl to say goodbye to her parents when Rainbow White appeared to comfort her. She wrote a poem. Should I recite it?" Ming nods yes and Ma Fun does.

"Rainbow White

Keep me safe day and night

For my family is gone from sight

Be my sun and moonlight, dear Rainbow White."

Ming listens, and before he knows it, he is crying. The two holy men watch the grief moving through the boy's body, and they surround him with love and compassion.

When the tears subside, Ming says, "Tell her it is a beautiful poem."

"The girl's name is Yao Wei Lee, and she is waiting for me. I'm her guardian," says Ma Fun.

Li Wu tells Ming that the flying creature is a phoenix that represents the empress, while the dragon represents the emperor. When Ming shares that Rainbow White took the gingko plant, Li Wu laughs. "Dr. Chi Yu will be so delighted!"

The trio arrives at Dr. Chi Yu's house, and they are invited to dinner and to stay the night. The Shaolin priest Ma Fun expresses his gratitude and explains he must get an early start in the morning. While Mrs. Yu prepares dinner, Dr. Yu takes the three to his lab.

Upon entering the lab, Ming immediately spots gingko plants. The two holy men are surprised that the doctor wastes no time. He begins the boy's training by asking him to touch each plant. Ming reaches for the first plant and feels energy pulsating through his body. Each plant feels different. On the last plant, Ming lifts and shakes his left foot.

"What did each plant say to you?" asks the doctor.

The boy gives an accurate account of the health of each plant. "The last plant hurts here," and Ming points to the left side of the plant.

"Fascinating," replies the doctor. He empties the plant from the container and, sure enough, on the left side the roots are knotted in a ball.

Ming's new life fills up quickly. He becomes an apprentice to Dr. Yu and assists him with his practice. People come locally, nationally, and internationally to be treated by the medical herbalist. Those who come from far away stay at the Taoist Monastery, which brings financial support to both the doctor and the monks. Soon Mrs. Yu discovers that Ming, like herself, has an ear for languages. She observes he is able to pick up quickly the various dialects in the region. Ming loves the international visitors and the different sounds their languages make. Li Wu and Dr. Yu foray with Ming into the sacred mountains to find new species of trees and plants. Once they discover that Ming can draw, a sketchbook becomes standard equipment. Ming practices his drawing on the bamboo trees near Dr. Yu's house. "It is good to draw on the bamboo, for it symbolizes eternity," says Dr. Yu.

When they go looking for the plants and roots for their medicinal properties, Ming learns about the tree peony and finds new species of azaleas, rhododendrons, roses, lilies, magnolias, chrysanthemums, and camellias, which they carefully record. Ming is instructed to mark the location so they can return. Sometimes, Ming will remove the youngest and healthiest plants so that Dr. Yu can experiment and create new varieties.

Ming captures the plant's essence through his sketches. The recorded images are shared with their annual visitor, Dr. Laurence Edward. Dr. Edward is an Englishman, who looks for rare flowers for a number of English garden societies. Dr. Edward is so impressed with Ming's drawings that he gives Ming a set of colored pencils so that Ming might bring even more life to his drawings of the new varieties of rhododendrons or roses or camellias or lilies. Dr. Edward's annual visit brings additional financial rewards and a special friendship to Dr. Yu, Ming, and the Taoist Monastery.

When Ming and his two companions come across two chopped-down redwood trees, Ming cries. "Oh no, I wasn't here to protect them."

"Protection comes from an open heart and mind," advises the monk. "Go stand next to the tree that still lives."

Ming does and is surprised. "The tree is."

"A tree's nature is balance," adds Dr. Yu.

"Only humans can choose to keep their hearts open or closed," says the monk.

Dr. Yu senses the boy's confusion. "Trees live in the moment. Balance lives in the moment."

Li Wu adds, "And that is why when we stand quietly by the trees, we feel refreshed. The trees remind us to be in balance."

"Balance is what it means to be a green warrior," says Dr. Yu.

"But I hurt when trees are hurt," replies Ming and feels his heart closing, and he remembers his grandfather's words of how sadness will close his heart.

In the sacred mountains on a misty day, Ming comes upon a small hut. He draws it and it reminds him of famous images of a lone man walking or riding into the mist. But his reverie is interrupted when he hears the doctor calling him. When Ming arrives, he sees a very old man sitting and eating with the doctor. "Ming, this is a very special person. He is 502 years old."

"My grandfather told me about you! How do you live so long?"

The Old Hermit laughs, "It's only one day. How old are you?"

"I'm eight."

"When I was your age, I planted so many seeds of the Dawn Redwood trees. They shared their secret with me. They live in the moment," says the hermit.

Ming remembers the cut-down trees and cries out, "But people cut them down!"

The Old Hermit reflects. "That's why my father had me plant so many! They support the planet by giving oxygen. The secret to a long life is to live like the Dawn Redwood trees. And you might want to add some joy and cheerfulness too." A look of surprise comes over Ming's face. His grandfather already knows the secret to a long life!

News arrives that Grandfather Mee isn't well. Dr. Yu and Ming travel to see how they may help. As they enter Grandfather's room, they recognize the signs. Ming touches his grandfather and feels his life force leaving him.

"Gung-gung, I met the Old Hermit who is 502 years old. He and his father planted the Dawn Redwood trees. He told me the secret to a long life is being cheerful!"

Grandfather laughs. "Ming, I have itchy feet. It's time for me to move on."

"But what about the family and what about me?"

"Ming, at eleven you already know many secrets and stories. The family does, too." Grandfather looks into Ming's heart and realizes there is one more thing to share with his grandson. "You have the Mee's curse of caring too much! That's why sadness affects you. Stay in the moment. This will help. You will feel me there." Ming sees his grandfather drifting away and in a soft voice his grandfather whispers, "The adventure never ends."

Ming whispers back, "Gung-gung, I'll miss you." Ming sees his grandfather looking up and knows he has left his body. Ming goes outside, sits under the willow tree, and cries. He leans into the tree and feels the tree's energy flowing through him. Balance returns.

A message arrives from Dr. Laurence Edward, urging his friends to leave the mountains and to come to Hong Kong. He informs them that with World War II being over, the internal power struggle for China will turn brutal. He advises them to leave China before the border crossings are permanently closed. Ma Fun and his ward, Yao Wei Lee, pull up in a Ford half-ton pickup truck to pick up Dr. and Mrs. Yu, Ming, and Li Wu and take them to Hong Kong. Dr. Yu and Ming put the finishing touches on the manuscript of the collections of healing plants from the sacred mountains of Southwest China. Seeds have been gathered and labeled. A wild rose plant is packed for traveling to Dr. Edward.

Ma Fun drives and Dr. and Mrs. Yu sit up front. Li Wu, Ming, and Yao Wei sit in the back with the luggage. Ming asks, "Will the trees be all right with us gone?"

"A few monks will remain behind, and the manuscript you and the doctor have completed will help," replies the monk Li Wu.

Yao Wei Lee observes Ming's energy. She sees heaviness. Yao Wei leans toward Ming and says, "When I was twelve years old, I learned that my parents might have been betrayed by a trusted relative. I wanted confirmation, but Ma Fun stopped me. He told me revenge was poison, but I wouldn't listen. The anger ripped at me until I got very sick."

"My grandfather once told me that caring too much runs in my family," responds Ming.

"Ma Fun has told me many times that I can learn through his words or through direct experience. The latter he tells me is the hard way," she says with gentle firmness.

"Well, Ma Fun has always been very wise," says Ming.

"Ma Fun tells me that the heavy feelings will go away if I don't relive them. My job is to bring awareness to my emotions and then decide what I want," informs Yao Wei.

Ming listens and then a smile spreads across his face. "Yao Wei, aren't you the author of the Rainbow White poem?"

She laughs, "Rainbow White is an amazing, magical creature. And if I remember correctly, you are a green warrior. You feel plant energy! I am just a warrior."

They stop for a rest and a bite to eat near the Summer Palace of the Mongolian Emperor when they see a pheasant flying over.

"We have witnessed a rare and wondrous moment!" says Ma Fun.

Ming gazes at the bird and glances at Yao Wei.

Li Wu and Ma Fun exchange looks and Ma Fun asks, "Ming, have you figured out the meaning of the dragon and the phoenix for you?" Ming blushes, but doesn't answer. He turns away so that Yao Wei can't see him. If he hadn't turned away, he would have seen her crimson face.

As they passed Yunnan City, Yao Wei shields herself with her breath and focused mind. She notices Ming's shield is unstable. Li Wu notices too and says, "Ming, trust that all are traveling their paths. Expand your perspective or you'll fall out of the present moment and close your heart."

"Am I so easy to read?"

"Yes," reply Li Wu and Yao Wei.

"Ming, we will be at the border soon," says Li Wu and nods to Yao Wei to prepare herself.

When they arrive at the border, Ma Fun explains to the guards that this truck belongs to an American. The American was studying at the monastery when the Japanese bombed Pearl Harbor. The American left China, enlisted in the war, and left the truck in his care. The American is now in Hong Kong waiting for his truck.

Dr. Yu hands a letter from Dr. Edward inviting him to Hong Kong for a symposium on healing herbs. The guard studies the group. The group breathes in unison, putting a shield of protection around them, but Ming fights for a calm mind.

The lead guard responds to the weakness in the shield. He shouts for all of them to get out of the vehicle and then peppers them with a series of questions: Where did they come from? How are they going to return with no vehicle? How many communists' gangs did they encounter?

In a calm, modulated voice, Ma Fun answers the guard's questions. Ma Fun directs the group's energy to counteract the guard's agitated energy. The guard heads to the back to inspect the truck. He surveys it, then uses his rifle to reach for a soft piece of luggage and pulls it toward him. He opens the bag, turns toward the group, and asks, "Who does this bag belong to?"

A nervous Ming raises his hand, and the guard motions him to come forward. The group remains tranquil, sending supporting energy to Ming as he walks toward the guard. When the guard pokes his finger in Ming's chest, a surge of dark energy shoots out. Ming stutters, but manages to explain that this bag is filled with healing plants and seeds for the symposium. Since he is Dr. Yu's apprentice, he is in charge of this bag.

The guard motions for him to open the bag. Ming's hands are shaking as he unfastens the bag. The guard asks Ming to pull some of the herbs out. Ming reaches in and brushes against the Dawn Redwood seeds and the energy of the seeds shoots through Ming as he hauls out a dried chrysanthemum. The seeds bring the Old Hermit to Ming's mind and he falls back into the present moment.

The guard makes a face and utters, "Hmmph." He stares at the plant and pauses a moment. He calls to his comrades to watch the group while he takes Ming and Dr. Yu over the tiny hill behind the guardhouse. Fifteen minutes later, the group sees three heads emerging over the hill. The guard is talking intently to Dr. Yu, with Ming carrying a plant with root hanging and with bits of dirt falling off.

The guard shouts to the group to leave. Ming climbs in the back of the truck and pulls out his sketchpad. "The guard's grandmother simmered the roots of this plant whenever he had a cold and a scratchy throat. Dr. Yu thinks it's in the primula, or oenothera biennis, family and he wants me to draw it."

Yao Wei offers to hold the plant.

The group arrives in Hong Kong and learns that Dr. Edward has been knighted by the Queen of England for his assistance in the war. Sir Laurence Edward is delighted by the wild rose plant. He informs Dr. Yu of their future in England and the likelihood of getting their manuscript published there.

Li Wu and Ma Fun linger until Ming and Yao Wei marry. Li Wu says to Ming, "Although this portion of our time together is over, our energies are forever linked." Ming feels sadness, but releases it. He knows that sadness lives in the past, and he wants to live in the moment.

Ma Fun says to Yao Wei, "There is nothing in China for you. Your path heads to the West and mine in a different direction. Journey well, my beautiful Golden Phoenix."

Yao Wei whispers quietly to her mentor, "I shall never forget you."

After the two holy men depart, Sir Laurence begins to acculturate the remaining group to a Western culture. He takes them to see an American cowboy movie starring John Wayne. He suggests they might consider taking on English names.

Privately, Ming recommends plant names like Jasmine, Ginger, and Rose to Yao Wei. She sneezes after reading about the spice, pepper, and she decides it's a sign. When she learns that black pepper is good for stimulating the energy flow, she is thinking she has found her name. But when she asks Sir Laurence if pepper grows in England, he replies, "No, but it is a favorite spice. I think pepper suits you."

"I think so, too," says Dr. Yu, who doesn't share that pepper also represents "spirit" or "energy," which he observes Yao Wei indeed possesses.

Ming announces, "Do you like Pokeweed, Yucca, or Alfalfa for me?" Pepper frowns and Dr. Yu and Mrs. Yu laugh. "Only kidding," says Ming and admits he is smitten by the cowboy movie actor John Wayne and would like the name John.

Sir Laurence didn't have the heart to tell Ming that John Wayne's real name was Marion. With enthusiasm, Sir Laurence says, "John is a fine English name."

Pepper gives Ming the "look" and he sheepishly says, "We will find good plant names to fit our children."

Pepper says, "Hold to your promise or no more American movies for you."

❦ 2 ❧

Angelica Isatis Mee:
A Donkey and a Thief

Dr. Yu's knowledge of plant medicine provides an opportunity for Eastern and Western medicine to join together. Dr. Yu and John Mee work beside a team of traditional doctors in diagnosing and treating patients at a local clinic. John Mee earns a doctoral degree in plant biology at Oxford University.

Mrs. Yu and Pepper Mee begin teaching tai chi classes at the university, community centers, and senior centers. Dr. Yu recommends to the patients and the doctors at the clinic to incorporate tai chi for health purposes. "Plants provide balance. Tai chi moves energy for balance," says Dr. Yu.

When *Healing Herbs of the Chinese Civilization* by Dr. Chi Yu and Dr. John M. Mee is published, Stanford University invites Dr. Yu to come and participate in a special grant for investigating the medicinal properties of plants in America. Dr. Yu turns down the offer and suggests John Mee in his place, which upsets Mrs. Yu. "John and Pepper are our only family now. How can you send them so far away?" asks Mrs. Yu.

"It's a good grant. Besides, how can I deny John the opportunity to visit the land of John Wayne, his namesake?" says Dr. Yu teasingly.

"All that poor boy has done is say goodbye to people he loves," says Mrs. Yu.

"Is that not life? Besides, he has Pepper like I have you," says Dr. Yu.

Two months after arriving in Palo Alto, California, Pepper announces she is pregnant. John keeps his word to look into plant names. As the leaves turn colors on a crisp fall day in October, Angelica Isatis Mee comes into the world. John proudly informs Pepper, "Angelica *atropurpurea* . . . the root aids in well-being and mental harmony and good digestion. The long, dark leaves of the isatis plant are an astringent to stop external bleeding. This plant is prominent in England and in America. And we have our own first aid kit." He holds up his daughter. Pepper rolls onto her side and falls asleep.

Two and a half years later, just when winter gives way to spring, Rue Comfrey Mee arrives. John holds his son up. "The rue plant expels poisons and the comfrey herb heals the lungs. And don't you like the way the two herbs sound together?" Pepper extends her hand for the baby as it is time to feed him.

Pepper uses her skill of astute observation on her children. She sees her infant daughter, Angelica, is defenseless against the moods of others. She shares this information with her husband who says, "She is like me! She has the Mee's family curse of caring too much. We will need to rely on herbs and nature until she can master her gift of sensitivity."

Pepper nods, remembering the border-crossing incident. She eyes him and wonders how many curses have been inflicted on the Mee lineage. She knows of wanderlust and sensitivity. Then a smile crosses her face as she remembers how Ma Fun managed to appear out of nowhere and always at the moment when she was caught between the old and new worlds. She knows he loved her unconditionally, but was persistent in moving her forward. She will do what he did.

When *Healing Herbs of the Chinese Civilization* is published in Spanish, the Mee family is off again. They live extensively in Costa Rica, with shorter stays in other Spanish-speaking countries.

In Peru, John learns from a Machinguenga elder, a medicine man, different combinations of herbs for healing, which Pepper gathers for her daughter. Recently, she notices her three-year-old daughter refuses to smile until her out-of-sorts playmates smile. Pepper holds her daughter softly and gently massages her tight little body. Then they take her and Rue to the rainforest and stay until the power of the natural world heals her.

Like a hawk, Pepper observes her children. A neighbor drops by and shares her woes of her husband being hurt in a brawl. Five-year-old Angelica absorbs the emotional energy and sinks into sadness. After the neighbor leaves, Pepper finds Angelica asleep while Rue is playing.

Pepper teaches her children tai chi movements as a way of instructing them how to listen to the rhythmic pulses of their bodies. Pepper observes Angelica's energy shift when she comforts the daughter of a Russian scientist who is upset. Pepper seizes the moment and whispers into the ear of her ten-year-old daughter, "Angelica, listen to your body." Angelica complains she is too tired and can't focus.

Pepper discerns that John seems to be having success in sharing parables with his twelve-year-old daughter. So Pepper comes up with a metaphor. "When we carry the pains of others, we become a beast of burden."

"Are you calling me a donkey?"

"Well, when something weighs you down, the heaviness throws your body out of balance. Can you feel it?"

"No, not again!" answers Angelica.

"Carrying is a devious business. You can't see when people throw their dirty emotions on you. And yet, like a thief, you take what is not yours and carry it."

"Mah-mee, first I am a donkey, now I am thief. What can I do?" asks Angelica.

"Listen, but don't carry. People are strong enough to carry their own burdens. Here is a secret I've learned. Every time people meet, there is an energy exchange. Let them match you instead of you matching them. If you are happy, stay happy until that person becomes happy."

"But what if that person is too upset to become happy?" asks Angelica.

"In that situation, it's best to move far away until you're strong enough to not be affected."

Angelica is impressed by Pepper's observational skills and decides to emulate her mother. She practices on Rue. Rue is practicing math in the dirt. She watches as Rue gets up and walks around, looking at the problem from as many angles as possible. Before she knows it, Angelica shifts from observing to helping, which irritates Rue.

Pepper, the master observer, steps from a hidden spot and confronts her daughter. "Did your brother ask for help? He may be younger than you, but he is very capable. When you deny him the opportunity to discover his own unique abilities, you deny him the opportunity to develop strong muscles."

Angelica cries to her mother, "I love my brother. I don't want him to struggle. Mah-mee, you always show up the moment I slip up. I feel like a big mistake!"

Pepper sighs and realizes how hard it is to guide someone. Immediately, she softens her tone. "Angelica, you're not a mistake. Your sensitivity to emotions makes you believe you are responsible for fixing things that belong to others to do."

"Will I ever get there? Will I ever learn?" whines Angelica.

"You're fourteen and *no one* masters one's gift overnight, so patience would be helpful here. Don't let the false belief of perfectionism rule you. That kind of thinking leads to judgment, which undermines your worth. And then what happens to the joyful attitude of learning? Gone, I tell you."

Angelica laughs and feels the tension leaving her body. Suddenly her shoulders and back relax, and she takes a long, deep breath and feels the peace.

Pepper smiles. "When your gift of sensitivity blossoms fully, I promise you will be freer than you've ever known."

Angelica studies how her mother handles emotional energy. They are at a community event when a woman complains about her worthless son. On their way home, Angelica asks, "You make shifting energy so easy. How do you do that?"

"I listen with empathy, not with sympathy. I don't pity her. I believe in her. I know she has the ability to change and make a different choice."

Angelica mutters, "She is strong enough," and feels her body responding. "My job is to believe in her," and a peace comes over her.

Pepper smiles. "The seed of Dawn Redwood tree has taken root in my daughter."

The Mee family declines an invitation to attend a Catholic service, and Angelica asks, "Why do we resist church?"

John and Pepper answer Angelica's question by taking the family into the rainforest. When John finds a good spot among the plants and trees, he says, "Let's experiment. We'll go into the inner realm of silence and see what happens."

John touches the plant world. Pepper picks up on a breeze. Rue and Angelica close their eyes and sit quietly. John and Pepper focus on their breaths together and then match the breaths of their children.

Angelica takes several deep breaths when a surge of emotional energy emanates from the mid-section of her body. She sees three tiny balls from her body moving in concentric circles, swirling into one golden ball of energy that intersects with the natural energetic forces of the rainforest that forms a canopy of pure, white light. At that moment, she feels she is everywhere and yet herself.

Angelica opens her eyes to see Rue fill with excitement. "A swirl of energy came and swept me up. Then I saw the center; the calmest, safest place. I thought myself there and there I went!"

"Rue, you have great intuition. You're so adept in the invisible realm! Angelica, it's your turn," says her father.

Angelica describes her experience and her father says, "Aaah, you have touched an invaluable truth!"

Angelica can't grasp the totality of her father's words, so she asks, "Ba-ba, did you know what would happen to Rue and me?"

"There are no expectations in the present moment." John is surprised by his own words.

Pepper jumps in, "There are many paths to the top of the mountain, and the church is just one available path. Wisdom, through stories, is infused in all cultures."

John listens and waits. "Now you have experienced the wondrous vibration of all things. We are separate, and yet part of all things. All is accessible to you. The door-way is the joyous, intuitive heart that lives in the peace of the present moment."

Pepper concludes, "Our teachers taught us Eastern beliefs, but they value all paths of thoughts. We hope you will take old thoughts and provide your own unique twist."

John laughs, "My beautiful children, you are the true wonder of the world. A wise world needs children's magic, their sense of wonder and delight. My grandfather says it's a Mee family secret—a loving, cheerful attitude makes for a joyful life." Pepper notes another family secret and at least he didn't say it was a family curse.

Pepper and Angelica are walking home with the wife of a visiting fellow scientist from Australia, Mrs. Anderson, and her daughter, Shirley. Angelica and Shirley are far ahead. They reached the place where their paths sepa-rate and wait for their mothers to arrive. "Angelica, you should be a psychologist. My friends don't listen. They just want to tell me what to do!" says Shirley.

Alone with Angelica later, Pepper shares, "Your energy is good and balanced."

Angelica smiles. "Mah-mee, I saw her!"

"You have changed your challenge into a gift."

"I just listened. It's so easy. I love it!" beams Angelica.

"There is another gift even more extraordinary," says her mother.

"What is it?"

"You must discover it for yourself. Every child has it," hints her mother.

With great resolve, Angelica declares, "Then I will find it, even if it takes me my whole life to do it!"

"It won't take you that long." Pepper wonders if Ma Fun had a similar moment with her.

An idea pops into Angelica's mind. "I know what it is. It's me!"

John presents his daughter with a neon green canvas duffle bag as she heads off for college. His eyes water as he shares, "When I left home at six years old, my grandfather gave me a travel bag to fill with adventures. He told me that the Mee family has a history of itchy feet and cheerful hearts. Before he died, he shared a family curse of caring too much. I know how hard it's been for you, but you've mastered the curse." John's voice is buoyant. "Here's a secret I've discovered. The natural world of plants is a silent reminder to balance. If I am in balance, I am a healer. I am the green warrior."

"Ba-ba, every child should have what Rue and I have had."

"Then it is up to you to make that happen," says her father.

Angelica knows to match her father's energy. They laugh as images come to their minds of children exploring the rainforest, of an old hermit traipsing through the Red Dawn Forest, and of a dragon telling stories to children while flying over a lake. Angelica feels light inside, something joyous rising from the depth of her being, and she is excited.

⚜ 3 ⚜

Payne Ow Porter:
Truth of Indigestion

In the practice of quieting his mind, Payne Ow Porter feels a deep stirring within, sitting right on the periphery of his consciousness. Is he prepared? His anxiety escalates when he remembers his childhood friend and agent Scott Green's pleading voice. "Promise me you won't limit your talents to just academia."

Doubt has haunted Payne since childhood. He has tried picturing himself as an action figure hero, commanding his nemesis, self-doubt, to go away. To his dismay, self-doubt is an exemplary adversary that holds him by the scruff of the neck, creates knots in his shoulders, and gnaws at his gut. In his logical mode, he holds his parents' cultural heritages responsible for his insecurities. His parents met at Hayward State University, where they studied to become teachers. Payne may blame his cultural mix, but his birth at the beginning of the 1960s was a sign of the Cultural Revolution.

Payne is challenged by which ethnicity box to check. He swears someday he will create a box for "other." Payne is half Chinese, a quarter Black, and a quarter Native American. Perhaps that is what prompts people to ask,

"What is he?" His parents answer simply. "He is our beautiful son." They celebrate Payne's diversity by reading to him African, Native American, and Chinese myths, legends, and folktales.

Payne spends hours reading, seeking an answer to the question of how to banish self-doubt. As Payne grows older, he finds solace in the mystical books his parents share with him, but one day he almost chokes when he learns that he chose those two crazy people to be his parents!

In graduate school, Payne discovers the Swiss psychologist Carl Jung and his personality types. He identifies himself as an introvert, which explains why he enjoys hours of research in the library. It suits his interior nature. In contrast, his friend Scott is an extrovert, which explains his love of interacting and communicating with the outside world.

Payne surrounds himself with mystical books. All that sacred knowledge comforts him. He feels like he is sitting in the middle of a sand painting, creating an osmosis pathway from the wisdom within the books to him. For graduation, his parents give him two books, *Tao Te Ching* and *The Life of Milarepa*. They inscribe: "To our son, may you find hope and tranquillity."

In the the *Tao Te Ching*, Payne finds inspiration. *The Life of Milarepa* punches through him. Milarepa, a Buddhist lama, lives in Tibet around 1000 AD Milarepa's father is a successful businessman but dies while Milarepa is a boy. A trustee is appointed until the boy comes of age. He keeps mother and son destitute while spending the inheritance on his own family. Milarepa's mother is enraged and threatens to kill herself if Milarepa doesn't seek revenge through black magic. Milarepa learns black magic and destroys the village. He is grief-stricken and spends the rest of his days seeking redemption, which leads to enlightenment and magnificent poetry.

Payne inquires as to the reason for selecting *The Life of Milarepa* for him. His mother replies, "Milarepa's story makes anything you're facing a piece of cake, and aren't you glad your mother isn't a drama queen?" With a lighthearted smile, his father answers, "Teachers are not wealthy, and this book was on sale."

Payne takes pleasure in selecting one idea from each book he reads to integrate into his life. From *Heal Your Body* by Louise Hay, Payne recites aloud, "I digest and assimilate all new experiences peacefully and joyously."

With his doctoral degree in philosophy in hand, he can't wait to teach; and, yet, he knows the academic community is circumspect about mysticism. And then there is the dream to make a difference. Can he use his gift to bring dissimilar worlds together?

Tonight he reaches for Venice Bloodworth's book, *Key to Yourself (Opening the Door to a Joyful Life from Within)*. He chooses to meditate on a joyful life. He sits in bed, feeling hopeful. This evening, it takes longer to achieve the peaceful state because he has overeaten, causing his body to chug along, digesting the heavy load.

He persists until stillness comes, but the heavy meal makes him drowsy. He slides under the covers. Before he knows it, someone is poking him. He opens his eyes and sees a noble Chinese Taoist sage in an elegant silk robe and hat, who commands him to get up. "It's time."

Payne asks, "For what?"

"To live as you believe joyfully," replies the sage.

Disconcerted by the lag time between his brain and mouth, not to mention the scattered thoughts and waves of panic and doubt surging through him, he still manages to spew out questions. "Is this a dream or vision? Am I in a different realm of consciousness? Who are you, and are we related?"

"I am one of your ancestral guides; it is time for your Progress Report." Holding a checklist, the sage put a checkmark next to an item. "You're seeing in color—a very good sign of evolving consciousness. Payne, please step up to the Mirror of Truth and look inside. It's time to see what you truly want and why you don't have it . . . yet."

Payne feels faint. Is he having a stroke from confused apprehension? He peers around and sees the bright colors. He is giddy with delight. And to think he saw himself as a black-and-white dreamer. He flashes back on his choice to focus on a joyful life. He didn't miss the irony. He asks for joy and gets a test. With anxiety, Payne blurts out, "I don't test well. My Chinese side, my Black side, and my Native American side—no ethnic part of me tests well!"

"Stand before the Mirror of Truth and see the fruits of your labor."

Payne panics. *Here in the moment of my truth, I'm glued to the floor. I can't get to the Mirror of Truth.*

"I can hear your thoughts. You can will the Mirror of Truth to you or you can will yourself to the Mirror of Truth."

"It can't be that easy."

"Choose one and find out!" commands the sage, and he sees paralysis setting in. He softens his voice. "*Fear and self-judgment block your ability to move. Calm your mind.*" Payne does and finds himself before the mirror. Payne thinks the Chinese sage took pity on him and brought him there. The guide shakes his head. "I am not allowed to interfere with free will. The fact that you freed yourself is proof of your desire to change. I am only a witness to your Progress Report. Stop looking at me like I am trying to execute you." Then the guide laughs. "Humans can be so intense. One of your gifts is tenacity. You only need to set your sight to achieve it."

The mirror darkens and pulls Payne in; he hurtles down into a deep abyss. Terrified, Payne stiffens. Out of nowhere, a shadowy figure catches him. "Relax and be free."

"It can't be that easy."

"If trying hard were the answer, you would be there by now. Put down the judgment stick. You're enough."

Payne's mind kicks in. "Progress Report implies evaluation and evaluation is a measurement of pros and cons."

"Good and bad is about judgment. Evaluation indicates where you are with your goal. Judgment restricts you to a black-and-white point of view. Evaluation opens you up to shades of gray."

The shadowy guide releases Payne, who expects to fall flat on the ground, but instead he lands softly in a dark alley and enters into a poorly lit teahouse. A silhouette looms over him. Sensing danger, Payne braces for a blow to his head or a knife in the back, when he hears, "Knock, knock. . . . "

Payne answers, "Who is there?"

"Joy. Aren't you glad that I live in the light? Why do you look for me in darkness?"

Payne groans.

"Other people's opinions rule you. Release the wondrous child within and free the unique you."

Payne wants to hear more, but he is a child now holding his Chinese grandparents' hands. People are pointing at him and asking, "What is he?" Then he is with his father's parents and people are staring at him. Payne's emotions flash through embarrassment, shame, hurt, and pure frustration.

The scene shifts. He hears a phone ringing and picks it up. "Scott?"

"Yes, your manuscript—"

"It's ready." Payne wonders if that's true.

"I hope the author was the joyous you," says Scott.

Payne hopes his Progress Report is coming to an end soon. Payne is sitting in a van full of people and hears people talking about what a good time they had. The driver shouts, "Everyone is here. 'Seriousitis' must be left outside of the vehicle."

Payne is struck by the odd request, and "seriousitis" sounds like a dreadful disease. He hopes everyone is all right. His mind goes wild with questions as he wonders about his Progress Report: Is the Mirror of Truth a reflector of his truth or universal truth or both? So, where is he in regard to living a joyful life? His mind gives way to the emotions of doubt and insecurity, causing him to move into a full-blown anxiety attack. *WHAT AM I SUPPOSED TO REMEMBER?*

The wide eyes of the Chinese sage gaze at Payne. "The softest whisper is heard throughout the universe. Why the sonic boom? We thought you would be pleased with your Progress Report. Instead, you're hyperventilating."

"I apologize. I forgot. I pride myself in being truthful with myself. I'm disappointed."

"You have eternity. What's the rush? You are closer than you know."

"But I still judge."

"Yes. You compare yourself to others. A true comparison can only be with you. You are unique." Payne listens and remains quiet. "The opinion of others is why you hide and is the main cause of your indigestion."

New thoughts drop in, but old messages speak. "I've been working my whole life, and I feel I will never be done!"

"It's bitterer near the root. One yank, it's gone. That's why we're encouraging you to finish your feelings of self-doubt and unworthiness once and for all." The sage asks, "What does your Progress Report tell you?"

"I am close, but not done. I need to put down the yardstick if I want to live from joy." Payne stands in awe as the mirror turns to pure light. The Mirror of Truth experience reminds Payne of Disneyland's Mr. Toad's Wild Ride. He mumbles, "What a way to experience a Report Card!"

The Chinese sage advises, "Payne, life gives you a constant Progress Report. Let your child of wonder and delight play. Your gift of clarity is what your friend Scott sees. The elixir to heal your sensitive heart is humor. Your guides tell me that they haven't heard a belly laugh from you in a long time."

"I feel like a gigantic onion with endless layers to peel back," moans Payne.

"That's a playful image. Your humor peeks out," laughs the sage. "A regular practice of relaxation would be helpful."

"But I do daily meditation!"

"But not at the time of eating." The sage tells Payne that one of his guides wants to emphasize the importance that when people speak, it's about them, not about him. Only his reactions are about him. "And when this cycle is finished, you will begin another that includes love, joy, and laughter. Doesn't that sound good?" The sage grins warmly.

"It's all I ever wanted. So, the Mirror of Truth reflects my current state of consciousness."

"We call the Mirror of Truth, MOT, which is an emotional vibration reflector. Your guides have observed the fluctuating moments of emotional constipation and diarrhea, so they have decided to bestow upon you the Portal Potty Principle, which is a metaphysical waste station, where you can make a conscious dump of negative emotions!"

Payne makes a face. *Portal Potty Principle is witty, but not very dignified.*

The sage replies, "You hide behind being dignified. This playful metaphor will coax your humor out from under your seriousness."

Payne blushes and blurts out. "I am the one with 'seriousitis'!"

"Well, how would you describe someone who has the gift of clarity and doesn't enjoy his gift?"

Payne realizes that he did this to himself. He remembers the adage, "Be careful what you ask for." The sage concludes, "You ventured into the MOT, and you were presented with the Portal Potty Principle. Don't question the package, just trust it. The MOT experience will help you and others let go and lighten up. We'll send more remedies for your seriousness problem."

In a heightened state, Payne wakes up and hears the ticking clock reverberating through the stillness of the night. The texture of cotton sheets lies across his body. He finds his journal and writes feverishly. When he comes to the Portal Potty Principle, he halts. His reserved nature dominates and he muses: *How come I couldn't get a good phrase like, "Let Go and Let God?"*

The next day Payne honors his MOT experience by going to the barber shop and getting a new hairdo. He looks in the mirror and sees himself coming. He feels special, but when he thinks of the Portal Potty Principle, he can't shake the image of being laughed at and, even worse, being shunned by his peers.

Payne struggles with stepping into the light and sharing the full MOT experience or staying hidden in the shadows. Then a third option comes to him. He could camouflage the Portal Potty Principle. After all, whatever he sets his mind to, he achieves. He turns to his good friend, the latest edition of *Webster's Unabridged Dictionary*. He opens the dictionary and fingers down to the word *portal* and reads "doorway, sometimes figurative, as, the portal of wisdom." The definition melts his heart.

Payne goes to the word *potty* and reads "from the phrase *to go to pot* or from the notion of drunkenness was a British colloquialism for trivial, petty, or slightly crazy." The word doesn't fit; he throws it out. He goes to the word *principle* and reads "(Latin *principium*, beginning). The ultimate source, origin, or cause of something, a fundamental truth, law, doctrine, or motivating force upon which others are based." Feeling uncertain, Payne wait-lists it.

He slaps his forehead as the word *philosophy* pops into his mind. *I have a doctorate in philosophy, for goodness' sake!* He locates the word philosophy and savors each word like a lover—"originally, love of wisdom or knowledge; a study of the processes governing thought and conduct; theory or investigation of the principles or laws that regulate the universe and underlie all knowledge and reality; included in the study are aesthetics, ethics, logics, metaphysics, etc."

Payne likes: *portal* and *philosophy*. Moved by the rich symbolism of these words, he plays with them. The word *time* slides right between the two: Portal Time Philosophy.

Payne writes: "The Portal Time Philosophy is a philosophy of perceptions and the limitations they impose. In Plato's story of the cave, the people shackled inside believe the shadows cast on the wall to be the real world. They are afraid to go outside into the false light of the day. So the question becomes: Once perception is formed, can it be changed?"

Payne wonders about this question in regard to himself. He hasn't exactly turned his back on the Portal Potty Principle. He's just cleaned it up. Payne compromises by putting more vulnerability in. "For so long, mankind has controlled the masses with feelings of inadequacy, resulting in puffed-up egos. But if we are willing to examine our lives as Socrates advocated, the collective has a chance to balance rational mind with the power of emotions. Perhaps, the true self doesn't need to hide behind, or ride shotgun over, ego. The truth is: It isn't easier to remain the same than to change."

He edits his words and uneasiness creeps in, but he manages to push it aside. He quotes his favorite philosophers, which bolsters his confidence to present the Portal Time Philosophy. He feels secure that a professorship is in his future and forgets all else. Payne assures himself that his clarity of thought will help humankind. He seals his manuscript and mails it to his agent, Scott Green.

At the age of three, Scott and Payne met in a playgroup. Scott considers Payne his brother. They are an unusual pair and easy to spot. Scott has gray-blue eyes and unruly brownish-yellow hair and pale skin, whereas Payne has chocolate eyes, short, black kinky hair, and copper-colored skin.

Scott assists in getting Payne's book, *The Rhythm of Rest: The Role of Faith in the Shamanic Buddhist Traditions*, published. He knows his friend wants to write a scholarly book that engages rather than bores students. They put in as much life as allowed by educational publishers and the academic community.

Scott considers his friendship with Payne first and his role as agent second. They recently talked about unique ways of presenting truth. Scott thinks they make an excellent pair, with Payne's gift of clarity with lofty thoughts and his own gift of networking and promotion. When Scott reads Payne's latest manuscript, he is puzzled. The manuscript is again geared toward academia, which means it lacks mass appeal. The culprit, Scott suspects, is Payne's desire for professorship.

Scott knows Payne wants to make a difference. For months now, Scott has been sending out feelers for unique projects to come his way. When he came across Joseph Campbell, a liberal arts professor, he was beside himself. Campbell was impacting the general educated public and filmmakers, too! Scott senses the timing is right, if only he can get Payne to loosen up.

Scott's secretary buzzes him to announce that Payne has arrived and that Kate Newman is on the line for him. He and Kate have been playing phone tag, so he opens his office door and calls out, "POP, I need to take this call."

Payne figures this call must be important. Only Scott still calls him POP. Even his father doesn't call him that anymore. Life through his parents conspires to torment him. His father, Rodney, chose his son's first name: Payne, a symbol of resilience and clarity in glass and of endurance gained through fire. His mother, Shirley Ow, insistsed her maiden name be her son's middle names and POP became his initials.

For years, his father teased him in front of his friends, calling him POP. They thought it was hilarious and never tired of asking, "Want some pop, POP?" or "How about a lollipop, POP?" Generally, Payne didn't protest, but merely sighed. Once he asked his father why he loved calling him POP. His father replied. "So you won't take yourself so seriously."

Scott does a double take before ushering Payne into his office. They share a similar build and height. Then Scott realizes what it is and chuckles to himself. Payne's hair is stacked six to eight inches on his head. "Cool new hairdo, bro. If only your manuscript had the same—"

"What, not enough mass appeal for you?" replies Payne.

Scott peers at Payne. "Are you hiding something from me? Confess now and I'll go easy on you."

"Hey, I thought had I found a middle ground where academics and lay people meet."

"Middle ground never works. Your hair screams, 'Look at me. Here I am!' Your manuscript says, 'Look for me in the stacks.'"

"How can you say that!" cries Payne.

Scott studies Payne. "Something is off. Are you familiar with Dan Millman's book, *The Way of the Peaceful Warrior*, a semi-autobiographical novel, blending truth with fiction?" When Payne nods his head, Scott explains, "Well, the call I had to take is from Kate Newman and they are looking for a manuscript along these lines. I told her I had an author who could do it and that author is *you*."

Payne pinches himself and Scott looks at him askance. Payne swallows hard and slowly launches into his metaphysical experience involving the Mirror of Truth (MOT), but leaves out the Portal Potty Principle. Scott can't stop smiling, especially when Payne tells him that he was in one of the dreams, and Scott says he looks forward to reading the manuscript in Payne's own joyful voice.

"Wow, an adventurous metaphor wrapped in a metaphysical experience—I love it! Your guides, and, according to your dreams, I'm one of them. But I'm telling you that the joyful voice is missing. Why is that?"

Payne is silent, so Scott probes further. "I can detect when you are lying to yourself. Make it easier on both of us and spill it."

"That's so unfair to use your supernatural powers on me. I worked hard to clean up the Portal Potty Principle," exclaims Payne.

"What's a Portal Potty Principle and why does it need to be cleaned up?"

With a look of angst, Payne explains. "The Portal Potty Principle is an emotional waste station where you take a cosmic emotional dump, releasing old ways and opening up to a new cycle of being."

Scott reassures his friend. "I use my intuitive abilities for the good, and I use my abilities on you judiciously. Does disguising the Portal Potty Principle have anything to do with the academic community?"

With a guilty look, Payne declares, "What college would hire me, let alone grant me full professorship, with the Portal Potty Principle?"

Scott is empathetic toward his friend while doing the happy dance inside. "Look, people pay good money to psychologists and psychics for the kind of services I share with you for free. Why do you give power to people you haven't even met? Vulnerability and humility make you real and that draws people to you."

"Now you sound like the Chinese sage," mutters Payne.

Scott pleads with Payne to share his entire MOT experience. Payne laments that he is a teacher at heart and he really wants a full-time teaching job. Scott takes a deep, full breath before he speaks. "Look, your guides believe you need a good belly laugh, and educational institutions have a terrible sense of humor. As I see it, you have been given an opportunity to bridge the divide between the academic world and the general population. Humor is a witty bridge. And what about your students— don't they deserve to be entertained as well as informed? Go home, have a good cry. Better yet, go to the Portal Potty Station. Flush away any fears, doubts, and negativity. Release your joyful self and write!"

Payne's ashen face tells Scott to back off a bit. He offers to find a home for his current manuscript and to help him land a professorship. Then Scott gives Payne another dose of reality. "Payne, I know how fond you are of Carl Jung. Perhaps it's time to deal with your shadow side. Be courageous. How do you like, *The Mirror of Truth: The Portal Potty Principle Revealed* as a title for your book?"

Payne admits he is filled with gratitude for the MOT experience most of the time. It is only when he thinks about sharing it with the world that he wants to throw up.

Scott goes into persuasive athletic-coach mode. "Don't let the self-conscious, serious, and dignified-ego part of you win. Bring life and humor to higher education. Bring levity back to learners!"

Scott stands up, encouraging his friend to do the same, but Payne doesn't move and asks, "So, am I to be the sacrificial lamb?"

"I am afraid so, and a bleating and whining one, I might add. Payne, I have suffered at the hands of unbalanced education—too much logic and not enough imagination. Step up to the challenge and take one for the humanity team. Be the spokesperson, the poster boy, for creative imagination." Scott shakes his head and laughs. "The potential for marketing lines is phenomenal. 'Is your life down in the dumps or perhaps in the toilet? Do you need a laxative for your emotional constipation? Go to the Portal Potty Station for relief.' That's just off the top of my head."

Scott slaps his thigh. "Payne, the MOT experience is the golden opportunity for reaching the widest audience possible. Don't throw it away."

Payne is humored by his friend's dramatic production. "If I volunteer to be the messenger of the Portal Potty Station, I'll shoot myself for not reading the fine print. Most certainly, I signed under duress."

Scott slaps Payne's back. "Complaining humor . . . that's the spirit. I am going to call Kate back and negotiate a lucrative contract. Payne, this is your agent and guide speaking: write from your joyous self." Scott pushes his friend out the door and promises to call him next week for a progress report.

Payne goes home and has a tantrum. Is his best friend's insightful gift a curse or a blessing? Is he really co-creating this situation? Can he really laugh fear away? Payne is on an endless loop. Finally, he hears his whiny, pathetic self. He hears the voice of the Chinese sage telling him to put down the measuring stick.

With release and acceptance, Payne retrieves his draft of the MOT experience as he experienced it. He allows his heart to lead and the words and wisdom to flow freely. He notices that the moment ego-voice appears, the creative juices stop. Payne finishes the manuscript at the same time that he lands a job offer from the state university where his parents met—much to his and their delight.

He feels being a full-time professor fulfills his life's purpose. He belongs in the academic world but is unprepared for the institutional games of being a university faculty member. His ethnic brothers and sisters point to the importance of affirmative action, which allows him to join their ranks. His Anglo colleagues point to his outstanding scholarship, indicating that affirmative action is no longer needed. Payne can see both sides, which makes being around both camps tricky. He suspects fear is present. Fear is notorious for separating people, and fear is certainly an equal opportunity employer.

Payne's father, as a high school history teacher and wrestling coach, motivates his son and students with the story of *Iron John* as retold by Robert Bly. A young boy falls into the monster-infested water and an ugly, hairy creature, Iron John, grabs and holds the boy. The boy struggles fiercely. The more he fights, the more strongly the creature grips. The boy finally lets go. The murky water becomes clear and Iron John becomes a healing force. Then it dawns on Payne that transformation is about moving through and beyond one's fears.

A year and a half later, Payne Ow Porter's *The Portal Potty Principle: A Magical Waste Station* is released and makes *The New York Times* best-seller list. With success, Payne faces his greatest nightmare. His academic colleagues warn him such a popular book might jeopardize his tenure. His colleagues are reluctant to help with teaching his classes and getting too close to what they perceive as popular culture. His teaching assistants cheerfully come to his rescue so he can do book tours.

Scott Green surprises him in Tempe, Arizona, by taking Payne to breakfast. "I was thinking about you the other day. I look at your schedule and what do I see? You're in Tempe at the same time I'm taking my folks to the Mayo Clinic just up the road."

Payne's stomach is rolling. He had a message dream this morning and here sits Scott Green. Once breakfast is ordered, Payne reveals, "I had a metaphorical dream this morning. I know you want to hear it, so here goes:

"I was in a woody area when I came upon a clearing and a special log cabin where thoughts are instantly manifested. I knew to seize the moment. I headed for the cabin, but a strong wind held me back. The harder I pushed forward, the stronger the wind became. I tired and rested by a small pond. As I stared into the water, a muscular arm emerged and pulled me in. I was dragged to the bottom by a wild, hairy man. My immediate response was to resist. To no avail, of course. Then I realized the wild, hairy man was Iron John and I knew to let go and hug him. Everything disappears and I am standing on the porch of the cabin. I know what I want. I reach for the door and wake up."

"Is this the first dream since the Mirror of Truth experience?" Payne nods yes. Scott laughs, "Amazing . . . Kate Newman recently inquired about a sequel."

"I am already unpopular with my peers," laments Payne.

Scott interrupts him. "Stop! We've been down this path before. You're not here for your peers' approval. The ugly truth is they're jealous and ugly Iron John is beautiful."

"I must be dense, because I keep getting the same messages over and over again," says Payne.

"Change is gradual. Your struggles tell people that you are writing from experience, not theory. We're moving toward the second printing of your book. The publisher has been inundated with letters, and they want to take a few for the back of the book jacket. Read these:

> Dear Payne,
>
> I love saying to my congregation, "No matter what life deals you, use the Portal Potty Principle for a cosmic high colonic, for a universal and complete royal flush!" It brings levity back to us all. Thank you.
>
> Reverend Jackie Garner

> Dear Payne,
>
> Your book can discharge any emotionally constipated person—at least it did me. Plugged up like you, I gave myself a good flushing out the other day. I read your book and laughed so hard, causing my poor pride to slump away. I now have hope for a better life. Thank you.
>
> Henry Rush

Dear Payne,

Bravo! You doused self-doubt with a heavy dose of humor. I've read many spiritual books and the majority of them are solemn, except for the Swami Beyondananda. Imagine my delight to find (from a professor, no less) true freedom's best friend is humor. I welcome any opportunity to use the Portal Potty Principle. Finally, the path to enlightenment is joyful. Thank you.

Faith Hart

A smirk of mirth spreads across Scott's face. "Great letters, don't you think?" Payne feels his shoulders and stomach tighten but tells Scott that he thinks the letters are clever and cute.

After breakfast, Payne decides to take a meditative walk. He allows his thoughts to come and go, when he spots a park with swings. Recalling how much fun it was to swing up high as a child, he makes a beeline for the swing set. He squeezes into one of the swings, but his legs are too long to get started. He debates what to do when he hears a voice from behind say, "Let me give you a push."

Unable to turn around, Payne simply responds, "Thank you!" He lifts his legs and, with a push, he goes flying into the air. With his own legs, he goes higher. Payne feels the exhilaration of being young and laughs and laughs. When he finally stops, he stands and turns around. He sees a petite Asian woman about five feet two inches in height with shiny black shoulder-length hair and delicate features. He smiles and thanks her.

"Your laughter is rich and deep and resonates with joy. I hope you exercise it often."

"Not often enough, I'm afraid." Payne leans forward and whispers, like telling a secret, "I've been accused of being too serious."

She matches his antics and replies, "Oh no! I think the trickster has a grip on you. Tricksters are known to dangle a protagonist in the most precarious dilemma like giving a serious, shy person a silly, flamboyant gift."

"That's exactly what happened to me!"

"Well, don't delay. Let the trickster's unpredictable approach free you. The real shame is that the trickster must resort to such tactics because adults have forgotten how to play. It's very sad, since children naturally know how to play. We all come into the world vulnerable, open, and free. Wouldn't it be nice if we could nurture our gifts from the get-go? I think the world would be a very different place."

Payne feels his energy shift; it is lighter. "So serious-ness is an adult attribute. I guess self-doubt is, too."

Payne observes the joyful light in the woman's eyes as she says, "Hey—I'm going to an author event tonight—Payne Ow Porter. He presents truth in a natural and pure childlike way. I was so impressed with his book that I'm bringing my protégé and my psychologist brother to hear him. If you're available, you should come."

Payne laughs, "Now I have no doubts trickster energy is about . . . you see, I'm Payne Ow Porter."

"There is no doubt at all! Your work is remarkable."

"Thank you . . . and you are?"

"I'm Angelica Mee."

"But of course you are. My metaphorical-metaphysical angel would be named Angelica!"

"Thank you for thinking I am an angel, but I hope you won't be disappointed when I tell you that I am named after a plant. I was raised by trickster parents and a long line of ancestors who believe the secret to a joyful life is an open mind and a cheerful heart." Angelica looks at her watch. "I better be off. See you tonight."

Payne remains a while longer. He sits down on the swing again and feels joy spreading inside him. He hears the Chinese sage saying to him that it is time for him to live as he believes. He closes his eyes and enters the Portal Potty Station. He realizes he is unique. His ethnicity prevents him from blending in. He laughs at the beautiful irony of life and invites his joyful self to come out and play. Soon he feels a sensation roaring up from his belly that comes out as a deep laugh, when it dawns on him that his guides had disguised the Universal Law of Attraction as the Portal Potty Principles.

Payne Ow Porter, alias POP, has finally popped open. He recognizes the cure for indigestion is humor. The angst of being different forced him to confront this issue early on in his life. The truth is everyone is different. Payne feels so light and joyous and understands the Negro spiritual—free at last, free at last.

⚞ 4 ⚟

Eviann Adams:
Secret of the Pink Light

Eviann asks, "What about all the other treasures?"
"Eviann, this is no time for using your imagination!"
shouts her father.

Her older sister whispers, "Only children can see the
treasures in the Cave of Reflection; even I'm beginning
to forget."

A familiar pink light appears and comforts her. The
pink light guides her to a parchment-paper book where
the pink light commands the snake, the single eye in a
triangle, and the triangle to leap off the cover page and
dance. The pink light commands the objects back to the
book and slips the book into Eviann's coat pocket.

Her father shouts, "Let's go now!"

Eviann places her coat inside her mother's hope chest.

A nurse opens the door and calls out, "Dr. Adams,
there is a patient waiting for you in Room 1."

Eviann Adams lifts her medium frame of five feet
five inches from the bed. She rubs grogginess from her
pixie green eyes and reshapes her massive curly auburn
hair. She is glad this is her last day of her ER rotation at
the Sydney hospital in Australia. In her fourth year of

medical school, she leans toward family practice. Before she reaches family practice, she has a pediatrics rotation.

Dr. Donald Nelson, the attending physician, is like the leader of a parade. He stands five feet eleven inches in height with dark brown wavy hair and a muscular build. He heads a team of physicians dressed in white coats holding clipboards. As the group enters the room of a sick child, Dr. Nelson, with a big smile, issues forth a hearty, "G'day." The child points her index finger toward one doctor. The interns follow the child's direction and part like the Red Sea, leaving Dr. Adams standing alone.

Dr. Adams watches the pink light dancing over the girl's tonsils, comforting the girl. This incident is repeated with other sick children, which embarrasses Dr. Adams.

Dr. Nelson pulls her aside. "Dr. Adams, you are like the Piped Piper of Hamlin. I hope you will consider pediatrics."

During her six weeks in pediatrics, Dr. Nelson, her supervisor, has mentored her. Over coffee and consultations, they have learned about each other.

Dr. Nelson sips his drink and asks, "Dr. Adams, your gift with children, how far back does it go?"

"I grew up near the outback on a farm on the outskirts of Deniliquin. My doctoring skills began with the animals on our farm. Willie, our sheepdog, had an eye infection. I was playing around with my stethoscope when Dr. Brown, the veterinarian, and my dad asked me to diagnose him. I pointed to the dog's infected eye. Another time they asked me about Billy, our goat. I told them the goat had a stomachache, and, sure enough, the goat did."

Eviann smiles, but doesn't share how she and the pink light developed a code: a bright, clear pink light means an area of health, and a dark pink light is the area of sickness. The pink light teaches her by scanning and slowly arriving at the problem area.

"I'm surprised you aren't a veterinarian."

"Dr. Brown certainly recommended that to my father. He treated me as a professional right from the start. 'Dr. Eviann, you must tell how you knew the goat was sick.'" She looks at Dr. Nelson and reminds herself to be careful around adults. He seems different. He is gentle and respectful of children. She asks the pink light to scan him, but the pink light is silent. Years of practiced withholding kicks in, "I told Dr. Brown and my father that the goat told me."

"Aahhh, the magic of a child's response!" exclaims Dr. Nelson.

"A story that gets repeated at every family function," says Eviann.

"Child magic, you can't beat it! It's what I love best about pediatrics."

Eviann thinks, *He gets it!*

Dr. Nelson and Dr. Adams know about the Sydney General Hospital policy of no fraternization between interns and attending physicians. The management believes the hospital will run more smoothly without emotional entanglements among the staff. They are mindful of the policy, but continue to share their visions for the future.

Dr. Nelson holds a mug of coffee. "Sydney may soon have a research center attached to a children's hospital dedicated to a holistic approach."

"What kind of holistic research?"

"The use of imagination or visualization in children's diseases like leukemia. Blending Eastern ideas with Western medicine. Eviann, what do you think?"

"What about children's intuition?"

"It would be a challenge to quantify. But that's what dreams are for." With a big smile and vibrant eyes, Dr. Nelson says, "Eviann, might that be a dream of yours?"

"Yes," replies Eviann, but all she can think of is *that darn no-fraternizing policy!*

Dr. Nelson writes a glowing letter of recommendation for a resident position with the Vancouver Children's Hospital in Canada. This hospital is dedicated to the care of children, using holistic methods to diagnose and heal disease and is linked to a network of children's research centers around the world.

Dr. Adams receives her letter of acceptance; she wants to share the good news with Dr. Nelson. From the doorway, she sees a huge banner with CONGRATU-LATIONS across it and spots Dr. Nelson embracing an attractive blond woman. When the blond lets go of him, he motions Eviann in. She waves the acceptance letter, but the blond woman intercepts her. "I just got engaged!"

People surround Dr. Nelson. Eviann never gets a chance to thank him or share her news, or congratulate him on his engagement. Her original excitement is diminished.

Eviann returns to the family farm. In the kitchen area, Evelyn, Eviann's mother, is cooking breakfast. Eviann puts place settings on the table and shares her excitement of going abroad but conceals her disappointment about Dr. Nelson's engagement.

Sitting and reading the morning newspaper are Robert, Eviann's father, and her older brother, Bobby. "Eviann, you must write a thank-you letter to Dr. Nelson," says her father. "It's not just good manners, but might be a ticket for a future job."

"Da, you're right. Networking is how jobs come about."

"It worked for me," chuckles her brother and Eviann shakes her head. Her brother always knew he wanted to be a farmer like his father.

Placing the plates of scrambled eggs and toast on the table, Eviann's mother asks in a resigned tone, "Must my daughters go so far way? Your sister is in London doing public relations for an opera company. You're off to Vancouver, Canada."

"Evelyn, what did you expect when you send your children to private schools?" inquires Robert Sr.

"Mum, this is 1987! Young people are going abroad to see the world before settling down. It's more than a hospital. It's a research center too," says Eviann, trying to console to her mother.

"It's true, Mum. Some of my 'uni' classmates have taken off," replies her brother.

"Just remember 'The Peddler of Swatham' story," says Evelyn as she launches into how the peddler observes a man waiting on the bridge. Out of curiosity, the peddler approaches the man and asks him what he is doing. The man replies he had a dream that a person would give him a message. The peddler laughs at the man and said if he were as gullible as him, he would be going to this certain village and digging under a tree by the old church where there is a treasure chest of gold coins. The man realizes the peddler is referring to his village. He thanks him and leaves immediately for home and the treasure.

"Even so, the man had to leave the village to find the peddler to tell him that the treasure was in his own backyard," says Eviann.

"Enough!" Robert shouts to wife and daughter. "The decision has been made. Let's enjoy the time we have."

Eviann writes a thank-you letter to Dr. Nelson. When the letter arrives at the Sydney General Hospital, the letter is forwarded to the Louise Parker Children's Research Center, where Dr. Nelson is now the new director of a center with a holistic approach. With so many congratulatory letters arriving, Eviann's letter gets jammed back into a corner.

The Vancouver Children's Hospital residency leads to Eviann's attending a conference at the Seattle Children's Hospital. The conference center is attached to the hospital through a corridor near the cafeteria on the first floor of the hospital. The theme of the conference is "New Approaches in Working with Children." All the sessions take place in a theater-style lecture hall with tiered seating.

Eviann arrives early so she can select a seat that is eye level with the speaker. She is thankful that the dress is comfy-casual. Today she chooses blue jeans, a periwinkle-colored t-shirt, a vibrant multicolored sweater from both the primary and secondary color palates, and then a light weatherproof jacket with a hood. This morning, she sees someone is sitting in the seat she wants. She sits next to him.

He eyes her. "What a colorful sweater!"

"Oh, my jumper."

Pointing to his name badge, "I'm Dr. Maxim Wright, director and founder of the Children's Learning and Diagnostic Center here in Seattle. I'm American and we call your jumper a sweater." Dr. Wright is in his mid-forties, medium height and stout in stature. His most noticeable features to Eviann are his warm, perceptive eyes, which embolden her to share how much she enjoyed his talk on the previous day and how much she looks forward to the afternoon visit to his center.

The two converse easily when Dr. Wright says, "Wait till you hear the morning speaker. You'll be over the moon with delight. She is a living example of someone nurtured from infancy."

"Good morning," says the emcee and the two stop talking. "Our speaker is Dr. Angelica Isatis Mee. Her father is Dr. John Ming Mee, the noted author and leading authority on plants as medicine. Dr. Angelica Mee is a doctor of pediatrics and plant biology. She is on the board of directors and a senior fellow at the Marcum G. Garver Foundation and Research Center in Tempe, Arizona, a nonprofit organization dedicated to promoting health in children—mind, body, and spirit. Please welcome Dr. Angelica Mee to the podium."

Dr. Mee steps up and begins her speech, "Thank you for inviting me to speak about a subject that is dear to my heart. I grew up in the rainforest of Costa Rica. My parents grew up in the sacred mountains of China. My father's teachers were a Taoist monk and a doctor of herbal medicine. My mother was raised by a Shaolin priest. Naturally, I was taught to listen.

"My parents loved to speak in metaphors. Here's a helpful one. 'Life gently whispers in your ears, but you don't hear. So Life taps on your shoulder, but you don't notice. So Life grabs a two-by-four and whacks you on the head and you say, 'What?' So would you like to listen now or listen later?

"Why is intuition so important? Intuition is quiet knowing. Intuition lives in the moment. Listening to my body taught me to listen and to be aware of my feelings and then my thoughts, which allowed my tiny voice of intuition to grow. Children, my dear colleagues, live in the moment. They just are. Their synapses fire on all cylinders with new discoveries. I'm sure learning how to navigate confining bodies would make everyone wonder, 'What have I gotten myself into?'" The audience laughs.

"In this noisy world, we see babies as clean slates with no imprint. If we can nurture children from the beginning and permit them to be free to live and dream from their innate self, instead of letting an unconscious veil fall over them, how different would this world be?

"The pores in our bodies make for healthy skin. Human beings are pores of the earth. Healthy human beings mean a healthy earth. The spirit of humanity is the child of wonder and delight that lives in each of us. This amazing gift from our creator needs to be nurtured.

"The Marcum G. Garver Foundation and Research Center is funding a research project on children's intuition. It is our hope that we can support Dr. Wright's work on the individualized educational plan based on the latest brain research and using assessment to fit each child's abilities and temperament. As project director and senior fellow, I will need a junior fellow to assist. If any resident physician is interested, applications are here at the podium."

The audience gives Dr. Mee a standing ovation. Dr. Wright nudges Eviann, "I have a feeling about you. I think you should apply."

Eviann heads toward the podium like a bee ready to pollinate a flower. It is difficult to reach the podium until the emcee organizes the doctors into a single line. Eviann reaches for an application when Dr. Mee asks for her name and her hospital association. Eviann feels hopeful, but her logical mind kicks in. *Don't make too much of it. She's being polite,* even though Eviann is aware that

Americans are not known for being polite, but rather for being direct.

Dr. Eviann Adams receives an acceptance letter from the Marcum G. Garver Foundation and Research Center and moves into the Desert Palm Complex in Tempe, Arizona. She is within walking distance of the research center. The complex has a community club house, a swimming pool, and a green beltway—a walking path.

On her first day, Eviann stands mesmerized by a wall of falling water in the lobby area. She doesn't hear Dr. Mee's approaching footsteps. "G'day, Dr. Adams. You found a place to regain balance and perspective. Let's begin our tour and get acquainted."

At the Learning Lab, Eviann can't believe the space. Angelica shows her how a miniature maze of chocolate mint plants and the tiers of plants of flowers, herbs, and vegetables can actually be outside by a push of a button where the roof retracts to let the fresh air and sunshine in. Since it is a beautiful morning, Angelica opens several windows. They pass a sandbox to reach a small pond with plants and fish, where they sit. "Dr. Adams, what do you think of the lab?"

"Dr. Mee, a mini-rainforest in the desert!"

"Call me Angelica, please. Children need nature to explore and wonder."

"That's what I did on the farm. Call me Eviann."

"This study is about children's intuition, so we will use our intuition in selecting the children for the study. We interview separately, but select together. Tomorrow we will have the opportunity to discover what innate abilities are obvious to us. The plants and the garden provide homeostasis for the children. Besides, intuition loves nature and will coax children's innate abilities to come out and play." Angelica caresses one of the leaves of the mint plant and laughs. "So, what events converged to bring you here?"

"How do you know?"

"Intuition loves to play with synchronicity." Angelica places her left index and middle fingers together to indicate the tightness of the relationship.

"I thought nature was intuition's playmate."

"Intuition has many playmates," says Angelica, with twinkling eyes.

Eviann can't resist Angelica's playful eyes and blurts out. "You were reaching out to me!"

"I knew you were the one. I had to get your information. I bet your logical mind interfered. But I could see that somehow you managed to block the unconscious veil from falling over you." Angelica explains the culture of the Marcum G. Garver Foundation and Research Center. Everyone cultivates their mind, body, and spirit through the practice of listening through meditation, yoga, martial arts, and journaling. They see food as medicine. "We put our findings to practice," says Angelica.

When they come across the state-of-the-art computer system, Angelica informs Eviann that the network system permits them to communicate electronically and by phone with colleagues across the country and around the world.

On the following morning, cheerful voices echo throughout the building. Angelica sits by the pond and Eviann by the garden maze. Eviann calls, "Patrick Edward Anderson." A little brown-haired boy of six with green eyes saunters up and says, "You have a pink light."

Eviann nods yes. The boy cocks his head to the left. "Can you move things around inside your head?" Eviann shakes her head no and puts a check by his name.

She calls out, "Rosemary Edith Dugan." A red-haired, freckled girl of five hops out of the sandbox and asks, "Does your pink light change colors like the woman over there? My favorite color is red, just like my name."

Eviann looks down on her sheet and sure enough Rosemary Edith Dugan's initials spell RED. She answers, "The pink light gets lighter or darker." Out of curiosity, Eviann points to Angelica and asks, "What are her colors?"

Rosemary throws her arms out wide. "A huge rainbow!"

Eviann places a check mark next to Rosemary's name and calls out, "Zaidee Lee Linch." A four-year-old girl wearing a baseball cap with Goofball printed across it appears.

Eviann smiles and asks, "Is that a special cap?"

"Special club—me," Zaidee points to herself, "Ryley, my dog, and my Grandpa Fred."

"What do you do?"

"We sing, dance, play, and, of course, watch movies!"

"Sounds fun. I like your name, Zaidee."

"I'm named after two grandmothers." Eviann thinks, *Can I put a check mark by everyone's name?* And puts one by Zaidee's name.

She calls out, "Matthew Andrew Dennis." A small boy with curly black hair and piercing blue eyes puts his arms out and gives her a hug.

Eviann feels his sensitivity to emotions, so she says, "My family is far away and I miss them." Matthew nods and Eviann thinks *he is too cute* and puts a check mark next to his name.

When Angelica and Eviann meet to compare their lists, Angelica's curiosity gets the better of her. "A number of children mentioned your pink light. Tell me about it."

"What about your enormous rainbow!"

"Rainbow White is a Chinese dragon, a symbol for emotional energy, a gift I had to harness. And your pink light."

"The pink light has always been around me. When I was young, we played doctor together with the animals on the farm. During my pediatric rotation, the children saw it. In fact, that's how I ended up in pediatrics." Eviann reflects a moment. "Do you think the pink light is my intuition?"

"That question certainly deserves your attention. Approach it from a child's perspective with wonder and delight. Document it in your journal." With a tender face and knowing eyes, Angelica says, "That's why you're perfect for the position." Eviann wonders what she means.

With the children selected and the study underway, Eviann ventures to the community pool. It's early fall and the weather is still warm. She comes to the pool gate and shifts everything to her right side: the water bottle goes into her hand, the towel is placed in her arm, and the book she tucks under her armpit, leaving her left hand free to open the gate. But the latch is stuck and she mutters, "Buggers!"

A male sits in a lounge chair and hears her. He is about six feet tall with emerald eyes and black collar-length hair. He opens the gate and says, "I haven't heard that word in a while. G'day, I'm Beauregard A Strickler at your service, milady, but my mates call me Bo." He bows. "I was reading the Green Knight and heard a damsel in distress."

Eviann thinks this is fun and plays along. She curt-sies. "I'm sorry to disturb you, Sir Bo," and rolls her green eyes in feigned embarrassment. "I'm Eviann Adams."

"Milady is most definitely from down under," smiles Bo. "You've been to Australia!"

"I lived in Canberra for a year. Aussies have a special place in my heart. Won't you join me?" Bo points to the empty lounge chair next to his.

Eviann decides to accept this invitation as an oppor-tunity to learn about American culture.

"May I ask what brings you to Arizona?" asks Bo.

Eviann explains she is finishing her residency at the Marcum G. Garver Foundation and Research Center. "This must be a special place for you to come such a long way," comments Bo.

She turns the conversation back to him, and Bo com-plies by sharing that his full name is Beauregard A Strick-ler, but that the middle initial, A, is just that, an initial. No period after the A, because his parents couldn't agree. He does not have a middle name, just a letter. Then Bo sighs and gives a look of angst. He explains his incom-plete name is problematic. If only his parents could have agreed, he would have a complete name and self-image.

Eviann doesn't have a middle name and can't fathom the distress in not having one. Then she wonders if he is pulling her leg. After all, she is unfamiliar with American humor. For now, she feels it best to leave his name issue alone, but decides to investigate her own name story.

Eviann is surprised by the pleasure in listening to people's stories. Bo shares stories about two men and a baby that he met in Lewes, Delaware, and his cousins from Tennessee. "Bo, you make the most ordinary people extraordinary," says Eviann. She looks at her watch. *Oh no, homework.* She thanks Bo for helping her with her assignment and excuses herself, but Bo delays her until she agrees to meet him at the clubhouse for tea and to hear her story.

Over tea, Eviann recaps the events that brought her to Arizona and exclaims, "There is magic in listening and speaking one's story."

"In one afternoon, you discover story magic. I am jealous."

"This is not a competition!"

Bo apologizes and explains. "It's my humor. You see, I'm an engineer/artist, and I'm beginning to see that's not a good combination."

Out of curiosity, Eviann asks, "Is this a new development, or have you always been like this?"

Bo shrugs his shoulders, implying he doesn't know. She wants to discuss this engineer/artist concept with Angelica. Perhaps there are other children like him. She asks Bo for permission to do so.

"I didn't expect to be a specimen and fall into your study, but if it means spending more time with you, that would be all right."

Flummoxed, Eviann turns to her science side and asks, "Which side came up with that conclusion?" Bo shrugs his shoulders again. Eviann persists, "Does it bother you that you don't know?"

"No, but I've noticed it can bother other people."

Eviann wonders if it bothers her. She decides it does.

Eviann accepts Bo's invitation for an evening walk around the complex. As they walk, Bo reveals all his failed relationships, ending with his divorce. Eviann feels awkward, as she is unaccustomed to so much personal disclosure from a person she hardly knows. She wonders if it is an American trait?

Bo answers her unvoiced question. "I'm sorry. I don't usually self-disclose so much, but there is something about you that pulls stuff out of me."

Eviann can't believe he blames her! On reflex, she shoots back, "I'm afraid you're the only common denominator in all these relationships."

"A shot right between the eyes. I guess I should be thankful you didn't suggest that I see a shrink," says Bo in a sheepish tone.

"But I do know a good therapist. My mentor's brother is a psychologist." Her sharp comments annoy her. This conversation is wearing her out. *Kind thoughts*, she reminds herself. Immediately an idea comes to her, and she tells Bo about Dr. Mee's husband, Pablo Mora, and his math camp where engaging math stories are used. Bo's eyes light up. Eviann offers and is successful in hooking Bo and Pablo up. When Bo thanks her, she feels disingenuous, because making amends is different from doing an actual favor.

Bo prepares a thank-you dinner for Eviann. He offers her a choice of white, red, or pink blush wine. He has had a few glasses of red wine and encourages her to catch up. Eviann looks at Bo's beautifully set table with flowers and lit candles and hopes their conversation won't venture into areas where she might step on his toes. She doesn't have any more ideas for making things right. She chooses the blush wine, and he tells her it will go well with the dinner he has prepared: pesto pasta, baby spring salad with balsamic vinaigrette, and fresh fruit compote with passion fruit and lime drizzle. After dinner, he prepares bush tea. She sits on the sofa and he joins her.

"Pablo is allowing my friend Dec and me to volunteer at the math camp. Dec is an educational consultant and on a mission to revolutionize education. I think this connection will be good for both Dec and Pablo."

Her motivation might have been wrong, but her instinct was spot on. A relaxed Eviann sits back and asks, "And what about you?"

"It's enough for me to tag along and see what happens."

"What about your dream?"

"It hasn't appeared yet."

Eviann can't imagine living without a dream. She stops herself from heading down the proverbial rabbit's hole by looking at her watch and saying she has an early morning call. Bo walks her home and kisses her goodnight.

On Sunday afternoon, Bo appears at Eviann's door and asks, "How ya goin'? Up for a walkabout?"

Eviann could use a break, but she hasn't had time to sort out the kiss and her feelings about Bo. He is an enigma to her. As she puts on her shoes, she wonders if this is really a good idea. Bo and Eviann walk in silence. Eviann thinks of Angelica's metaphor and wonders if life is tapping her shoulder in regard to Bo. Whenever she arrives at the whack on the head, she giggles.

Bo asks, "Want to share?"

"Angelica told this metaphor at a conference I attended. Life gently whispers in your ears, but you don't hear. Then life taps your shoulder, but you don't notice. So life grabs a two-by-four and whacks you across the head, and you say, 'What?' Angelica recommends it's best to listen now rather than later."

Bo doesn't say anything, but walks toward something. "This is spooky," and he points to two-by-fours lying in the recently cemented sidewalk.

"Oh—My—Gosh, it's synchronicity at play!"

"You don't think sharing a metaphor and then, abracadabra, a two-by-four appearing isn't a bit weird?"

"I love when unrelated events converge! Stop coming from your engineer side and let your artistic side out . . . just a suggestion, mind you." Eviann horrifies herself. There she goes again! She announces that break time is over.

As Bo walks Eviann back to her place, he says, "I love your clear thoughts. Perhaps the two-by-four metaphor might help me too." Eviann cringes and wonders what it is about him that unsettles her so.

Bo invites Eviann to go hiking in the Superstition Mountains. It is a favorite place of her mentor, Dr. Mee, and her husband. She wants to experience it, so she goes. She vows not to probe or engage Bo in any way that will cause discomfort. When they find a shaded spot, they sit and have a small snack. Taking a bite of apple, Bo says, "Logic would dictate that the pace of a relationship would have to go at the speed of the slower person, wouldn't it?"

Not knowing where Bo was headed, Eviann answers, "I guess."

"In our case, who would that be?" Bo asks Eviann.

Oh my God. Is he talking about us?

"I'm holding the two-by-four, and I'm doing the whacking," beams Bo.

Eviann hasn't figured out how Bo fits into her life. She really doesn't want to pursue this conversation, but here she is, so she opts for clarity. "Exactly what are you saying?"

"That we take our relationship to the next level."

In desperation, Eviann asks the pink light for help, but the pink light is silent. It seems she is on her own. She buys time by recapping. "You perceive me to be the slow one and that may be true. I am a feeler and feelers need time to take in all the information before they can make a decision."

"How long will you need?"

"A week or so?"

"Okay, take as much time as you need."

Twice now the pink light has been quiet. Both times concern relationships with men. Eviann considers the pink light might not have anything to do with her intuitive self. She asks for guidance from the still, small voice within. To her surprise a series of dreams comes. In the first dream, Eviann wears a pretty costume for a party in her honor. As she prepares to leave, she realizes all her material possessions were laid out in the open. Her instinct is to put them safely away. Her inner voice reminds her, "Trust. All you need is inside." She does. With her arm tucked into Donald Nelson's arm, they walk out the door with their entourage following them.

Out of nowhere comes a prehistoric animal charging toward her. The beast telepathically communicates. *Danger! Get to higher ground.* The animal veers off at full speed.

The dream shifts to a desolate, deserted place. There is a desert with miles of sand. She is alone. She notices a small depression on the ground. She goes to look and finds the prehistoric animal, sleeping in a comatose state. She gently prods the beast to rouse it. To her dismay, the slightest touch causes the animal to sink deeper. She realizes she can do nothing. She looks around, spots a mesa. She wants to go there and she does.

From the mesa, she has an excellent view. The animal never moves. She wonders how long she will wait. She becomes bored until she sees the pink horizon. Her desire to touch the sky is strong, so she leaps into the air with extended arms and flies straight up and pats the crimson sky and then wakes up.

In Eviann's second dream, she lies in a hospital bed, with Bo standing on her right side and another man bathed in pink light on her left. She places her hand on her chest and cries out, "My heart is broken!" Bo stares straight ahead. The man in the pink light moves her hand from her chest to over her heart.

In her third dream, Eviann floats about fifteen feet above the ground. She feels so light. As hard as she tries, she can't touch the earth. Standing on the ground is the man bathed in crystal-clear pink light. She hears, "Eviann, your dream lives in your heart, but comes alive on the earth. Come down and give life to your dream." The voice is both comforting and familiar. She floats gently down to the ground.

Eviann records her dreams in her journal and would like some feedback, but her mentor is away. So when Angelica finally returns and walks in with a book in her hand, Eviann blurts, "Angelica do you think dreams and intuition are linked?"

"I don't see why not, and what a fabulous question!"

Eviann has a fretful look on her face when she says, "I've had a series of dreams after Bo, the engineer/artist, asked to take our relationship to the next level. I've recorded the dreams, and I need help deciphering them."

"A series of dreams, you say. Why that's uncanny because the book I am holding is by Payne Ow Porter, who also had a series of dreams. Rue and I are going to the book signing tomorrow night. Why don't you join us? And I'll see if Rue can fit you in before going to dinner."

Eviann lets out huge sigh. "Angelica, you're an angel."

In the late afternoon on the day of Payne Ow Porter's book signing, Angelica and Eviann arrive in Dr. Rue Mee's office. Angelica shares that she gave Payne Ow Porter a push on a swing. Rue laughs and turns to Eviann. "This sort of things happens to the Mees all the time."

Eviann tells Rue about her dreams that came after Bo's request to shift their relationship to a more intimate one. Eviann expresses her hope for guidance. Rue complies. "The three dreams seem prophetic to me. The message is consistent. Do you know what it is?"

Eviann answers, "Something about my dream, my life."

"Where does Bo fit in?" asks Rue.

Eviann indicates she is unsure. Rue points out, "In two dreams, Bo is basically not present, very much like the comatose prehistoric animal. To me it is subconscious."

Eviann lets out a huge sigh. "Bo is nice, he's handsome, and tells great stories. But I feel on edge with him. I never know when I will provoke him to share things he normally doesn't. He doesn't have a dream and it doesn't bother him, but it does me." Eviann sighs. "I just can't be myself with him. He can't be right for me."

The two Dr. Mees nod in agreement and remain silent, allowing Eviann to take in her own insights. Then Angelica asks, "Do you know who the man in the pink light is?"

Hesitantly, Eviann responds, "I think he is a family member. I'm going to talk with my mum when I get back to Australia."

Rue says, "Eviann, you don't need my permission to listen, to trust your heart, or to live in the present moment, but I give it anyway."

The angst in Eviann's body has collapsed. So Angelica suggests, "I'm afraid if we are going to make the book signing for Payne Ow Porter, we need to go to dinner now. How does Restaurant Mexico sound?"

Eviann decides the best way to inform Bo of her decision is to cook a meal for him. Her place will provide privacy and safety for her feelings to be expressed. She makes a Caesar salad with blackened chicken breast and garlic toast. For dessert, she serves a pear almond tart. But her best strategy is plying him with liquor. After dessert, Eviann explains with the help of her dreams and Dr. Rue Mee, that she must focus and not be diverted from her dream.

Bo listens and adds, "I'll help and not distract."

Eviann feels irritated because she feels it isn't right to live another person's dream. She notes Bo's reaction, but decides to hold her ground. From the depth of her comes strength of resolve that is reflected in her words. "I would feel like a hypocrite if I allow you to do it. I need to model for the children to live their own dream."

"You're right. You're so far ahead of me. Can we still be friends?"

"Ahead of you? Again . . . you make this into a contest," says Eviann. She realizes Bo isn't arguing with her so she gives him a hug to cement their continual friendship.

"I didn't mean to," says Bo in an apologetic tone. "Are you sure you don't know my friend Dec?" Bo reaches for Eviann's hands and confirms, "Friends." Eviann laughs.

With her dream in focus, a package arrives from Vancouver Children's Hospital. Inside the package is a letter from the Louise Parker Children's Research Center. She opens the letter and reads.

Dear Dr. Eviann Adams,

I'm very happy to have finally received your note. Your letter was misplaced. I wanted to speak with you during the celebration party for the funding of the Louise Parker Children's Research Center. But my exuberant friend Tiff had just gotten engaged after waiting nine years for her Andrew to propose.

I knew the Vancouver Children's Hospital was a perfect residency for you. I'm excited about the innovative approaches you have acquired. I'm sure the children of Australia will be great benefactors.

As the director of the Louise Parker Children's Research Center and our sister hospital, Sydney Children's Hospital, I would like to offer you a position with us after completing your residency.

I've gotten permission to travel and visit the Vancouver Children's Hospital and hope to reconnect with you. I hear they belong to a network of hospitals and research centers that I would like our organization to join. I hope you will be able to assist me in making that happen.

Your ardent admirer,

Dr. Donald Nelson

Eviann feels giddy with delight. If she were a gymnast, she would be doing somersaults. She keeps repeating, *Dr. Nelson is single!* She can't believe how her subconscious mind knew. She loves how wondrously weird life can be.

An invitation is extended to and accepted by Dr. Nelson to come to Marcum G. Garver Foundation and Research Center in Tempe, Arizona, to visit the center and to meet with Dr. Angelica Mee. Driving out to Sky Harbor Airport, Eviann feels like a teenager with a mad crush. She stands nervously at the gate when a fearful thought crosses her mind. How embarrassing would it be if she didn't recognize him? But her heart beats rapidly the moment she lays eyes on him.

"Welcome to Arizona! You must be exhausted by this long trip." Dr. Nelson replies he feels great. Dr. Mee had provided an herbal travel formula and someone on his staff had given him an agate stone for jet lag. Eviann makes a mental note for her return trip home.

"No checked bag. I am ready to go and listen to what you have learned about children's intuition."

Driving back, Eviann explains that the Garver Foundation has several casitas, or small houses, for visitors. She blushes when she tells him that she is next door and has his key. She asks if he would like some tea, wine, or beer at her place. He gladly accepts.

Eviann pinches her finger. She can't believe that Dr. Nelson is sitting in her place drinking beer.

"Eviann, what is your favorite thing about children's intuition and healing?"

"Trusting intuition is an immunity booster." She can't stop smiling.

"This miraculous find may put us out of business." Dr. Nelson's eyes dance joyously.

"Should we be so lucky? There are too many adults who don't trust. We'll be safe for quite a while." Eviann doesn't want the evening to end, but she knows explanation can't match direct experience. "I think you should hold those questions until you've spent at least a day with Angelica."

"I will defer to you since you are the expert here. Since we will be colleagues, do you think you can call me Donald or Donnie or Don?"

"I can if you call me Eviann." Eviann pulls a key out of her pocket. "Donald, let me take you to your place." And they laugh.

Eviann leaves Donald with Angelica and heads for the children's lab. When the children's excitement level rises, Eviann figures Dr. Nelson and Dr. Mee must have entered the lab. Eviann goes to greet them, when she hears Rosemary Edith Dugan yelling, "Dr. Eviann, your boyfriend is here! The pink light likes him." This announcement brings the children running to investigate.

Blushing, Eviann walks toward the two doctors.

"A pink light?" says Dr. Nelson.

"The pink light can't move things around in her head," says Patrick E. Anderson, who pulls on Dr. Nelson's sleeve. "Can you?"

A smile crosses Dr. Nelson's face and he replies, "I believe so."

"I thought so," says Patrick as he hugs Dr. Nelson's right leg.

Matthew A. Dennis advances toward Dr. Nelson and, with his piercing blue eyes, says, "You be nice to her. She is far away from home."

Dr. Nelson bends down and says, "Well, I'm from her home country. We both live in Australia."

"Then you must be her boyfriend," says Patrick. The boy turns toward to Dr. Adams and shouts, "Dr. Eviann, he's a keeper!"

Now both Dr. Eviann and Dr. Donald are blushing.

Rosemary laughs, "My name spells RED, Edward's spells PEA, the kind you eat, not the kind you let out of your body, and Matthew's spells MAD. But I'm the mad one!"

Out of curiosity, Dr. Nelson asks, "Why are you mad?"

Rosemary tilts her head back, places her hands on her hips, and shouts, "I'm mad . . . simply mad, I tell you, with wonder and delight." The children immediately join in.

Throughout the lab, everyone can hear, "I'm mad . . . simply mad, I tell you, with wonder and delight."

Angelica laughs and addresses Dr. Nelson, "I'm sorry I never got a chance to introduce you to the children. How are you enjoying the tour so far?"

Not skipping a beat, Dr. Nelson, with gusto, says, "I'm mad, simply mad, I tell you, with wonder and delight."

"Children are so good at spotting one of their own. The Louise Parker Children's Research Center will be a welcome addition to our network," says Dr. Angelica Mee.

That evening, Dr. Nelson has dinner at the Mee household. Donald meets John and Pepper Mee and Angelica's husband, Pablo Mora. Angelica shares with her family the children's stamp of approval for Dr. Nelson. John Mee laughs and says that Dr. Nelson needs to be rewarded with a story of Rainbow White.

Learning about Chinese dragons only makes Dr. Nelson's curiosity burn. So he asks, "Does the dragon know anything about pink lights?" The room goes quiet and all eyes turn toward Eviann. Unprepared, she simply says, "I don't know! All I know is that children can see dragons and the children can see the pink light."

After dinner and over tea at Eviann's place, Donald and Eviann have a chance to process the day. Eviann turns beet red as she recalls the morning's events. "You know, when I said that you can experience for yourself what I've learned about children's intuition, I had no idea what would transpire this morning."

Donald, feeling a bit warm, says, "Obviously, children's intuition is magical as well as unpredictable. I love what happened this morning. What I like most about working with children is that they are so real and open. I hope someday I will be able to see your pink light, too." With a huge grin on his face, he says, "Besides, the Louise Parker Children's Research Center and the Sydney Children's Hospital don't have any policy against staff dating. I guess running a smooth, efficient organization isn't their top priority."

Eviann's eyes light up, and a huge smile crosses her face. Feeling relaxed, she says, "I'll ask permission from the pink light . . . and you never know. After all, I am still learning about the pink light myself."

With her residency complete, Eviann returns to Australia to begin her new job and to further her relationship with Donald Nelson. Her older sister, Trina, now works with the Sydney Opera House as the director of publicity. They decide to be roommates. The sisters receive a letter to come home for a visit. Trina arranges for them to take the train from Sydney to Albury and then a bus from

Albury to Deniliquin. Their parents will meet them at the depot and take them to the farm.

The conductor takes their tickets and learns the two girls are traveling home after being away. He lifts their tickets and say, "Cheers, mates."

Eviann responds, "No worries." Trina says, "No drama."

As the train starts to move, Trina reaches into her knapsack and pulls out a bag of biscuits. "Look what I found!" holding it in front of her sister.

"Tim Tams—the original ones!" cries Eviann.

"And in this thermos, Blue Mountain coffee," smiles Trina.

"Oh, so we're going to get slammed, are we?"

"What else are sugar and caffeine good for?" laughs Trina.

The two hyper sisters chatter from Sydney to Albury, trying to catch up on their respective lives. Heading toward Albury, the sisters crash. They are quiet and entranced by the sunlight and clouds altering the mood from one moment to the next. Eviann watches the light streaking down among the scattered clouds and treetops, creating a strange geometric design and then landing on a lone tree on a mountaintop. She utters to her sister, "It reminds me of the Snowy Mountains."

"Hmmm," responds Trina.

"Your warning about adults not seeing," says Eviann in a soft voice.

"Oh? I don't remember saying it. I hope it was helpful." Trina stares out the window of the train. Eviann looks out the window, too, and reflects. *It was a dream!*

The sisters are ready for a nap when they board the bus. When the bus pulls into the station in Deniliquin, the traveling sisters have tears of joy as they hug their parents and older brother. When the car stops, Eviann and Trina get out and hug the familiar gum trees that tell them they are home.

Everyone pitches in like old times for the family meal. Eviann and Trina prepare the salad. Her father and brother put chicken, corn on the cob, and fish on the barbecue and Evelyn makes a honey mustard vinaigrette dressing for the salad and a butter and garlic baguette.

They sit at the family table made of heartwood of pink gum tree that possesses shades of pale reddish brown. When Eviann spots a hint of pink, she makes a mental note to ask her mother.

The following day, Eviann and her dad drive out to the fields. She sees something she doesn't recognize and asks, "Da, what is that?"

"Rice. Your brother thinks it is good to diversify. The Asian market can't get enough."

On the drive back, they spot Bobby, Eviann's brother, moving sheep from one paddock to another. Father and daughter sit on the shed steps so as not to disrupt Bobby. Her father, Robert, looks at Eviann. "I miss my girls. You know you will always be my baby."

Eviann laughs. "Da, it's good to be home."

"Do you remember the trip to Yarrangobilly Caves? I was so worried. I'm truly sorry for being so cross with you that day. Eviann, I know you're a sensitive child, but for you to be so scared of me makes me ashamed and breaks my heart."

"Da, it is all right. Why are you bringing it up after all these years?"

"Well, your mum found something in your old coat pocket." Robert looks over at Bobby. "I think I'll see if your brother needs a hand. Why don't go find your mum and talk about the *Book of Life*."

"*Book of Life?*" Eviann quizzically says.

"Yes, the book that Great Uncle Ambrose went searching for," says her father.

Robert drives off toward Bobby, and Eviann walks off in search of her mother. She rounds the corner and passes her favorite gum tree with multicolored bark of deep beige, salmon pink, and sherbet green. Her mother spots her through the window and waves her in.

"Eviann, did you read the *Book of Life?*"

"No."

"You must. I want to know what you think. I've learned some interesting ideas," she says and hands Eviann the book. Eviann stares at the book. She sees a tree, a snake, and a single eye in a triangle. *It wasn't a dream!*

Evelyn misconstrues Eviann's interest. "Your Great Uncle Ambrose, I think, would make a good protagonist for a young adult novel. An Australian youth looks for adventure and travels to India and China seeking the mysteries and treasures of life, only to find the treasure he seeks is in his own backyard. How does that sound?"

"Mum, isn't that 'The Peddler of Swatham'?" Eviann accepts her mother will write a modern version of this story. "Mum, I want to know more about Great Uncle Ambrose."

"Well, he named you for Eve and Adam, a metaphor representing the beginning. He was an amazing medical intuitive, but rather pathetic with relationships. I was pregnant with you when he died unexpectedly. My mum begged me to honor Uncle Ambrose by choosing the name he thought up. I agreed, but I thought it only fair that if I use his name, he should watch over my child."

"Mum, he has. He put the book in my pocket. He's the one who helped me diagnose the animals on the farm. He's the reason I'm in pediatrics, which led me to Dr. Angelica Mee."

Evelyn tells Eviann to open the book. She does and the pink light fills the room. Eviann quietly thanks Great Uncle Ambrose for sharing his gift with her and for protecting her from falling into the unconscious veil of illusion, but most of all for his astute decision in letting her figure out for herself what she wanted and needed in a relationship. She closes her eyes and feels a joyous energy around her, the same joyous energy that she feels when she is around children who are exploring in wonder and delight.

⋐ 5 ⋑

Helena Sawolynska:
Race of the Charioteer

In colorful dress, an olive-skinned, dark-haired woman and her fourteen-year-old daughter stand outside a well-traveled trailer. The woman calls out, "Sophia! It's Sasha and Nadya Sinti."

A tall, slender, and dark-haired woman peeks out the window. She opens the door and invites them in. Once inside, Sasha whispers, "Could you do a tarot reading for Nadya?"

"Yes, since I won't be here again." Sophia explains her family has chosen to leave before the Gypsies, customs and practices are outlawed. She unfolds a card table, covers the table with a special cloth, and places three chairs around it. From a small wooden box, she gently lifts the tarot cards wrapped in silk. She holds the bundle and requests for what is needed most for Nadya Sinti to be revealed. The cards are spread out in front of Nadya. Sasha tells her, "Each card is a story, a symbol with hidden messages. Scan the cards with one hand and see which ones call to you."

Nadya points to two cards. Sophia takes them one at a time. "*Le Mat*, the Fool, is a wanderer who goes on the supreme adventure—to the gates of divine wisdom.

The Fool has much power and energy, enough to travel across centuries. See the blindfold. It means blind faith, so use your instincts. Fool is the zero number. It has no constraints. This card is tied to your lineage."

Sophia explains the second card. "This is an ancestry card too. *Le Chariot*, the Chariot. See the victorious warrior crowned and riding in a chariot drawn by black and white sphinxes? This means the emergence of a new guiding principle. The two cards together remind me of a story.

"Long ago in Alexandria, Egypt, there existed the most beautiful library in the world. A library filled with knowledge, with the mysteries of life. Scholars and priests managed the library. They were the keepers of the sacred scriptures. But as time passed, some people became threatened by knowledge within the library, so these people burned the library. Well, the sacred keepers carried away with them the most precious of the volumes (the Book of Enoch or Thoth—the Tarot). The sacred keepers became wanderers upon the face of the earth and remain a people apart with an ancient language, Sanskrit, and a birthright of magic and mysteries."

Tears came to Sasha's eyes. "Nadya, this is the history of the Gypsy people, our history."

Sophia continues with the reading. "Yes, you belong to this group and so will your children and their children."

"Since you mention children," says Sasha, "do you see a husband for my daughter?"

Sophia laughs, "I hear this question a lot. I do see someone standing beside her. He's tall and has a pale complexion. He's older and will provide well for her. Music will bring you together." Since the Sintis are musicians, no one is surprised.

Ivan Sawolynska attends the wedding of his assistant in a village outside of Kishinev. A young, exotic girl with wild, wavy black hair and tantalizing olive skin captivates his attention. Her posture is upright, making her seem tall, although she can't be more than five feet five inches in height. She stays close to an older woman and man with the same coloring, who he guesses must be her parents or relatives.

Ivan congratulates the groom, Dmitri Zakharov, and his new bride, Florica Zakharov. "It means a lot to Florica and me that you came," says Dmitri. "I know you love classical music, but wait until you hear some traditional folk music from the Sinti family. Nuri plays the violin and sings. Sasha sings and plays the tambourine, and Nadya plays the violin and dances." Dmitri points to them.

Ivan takes the opportunity to learn more. "The girl looks young, maybe sixteen."

"Music lives in our blood," replies Florica, "but she is old enough to marry, in our tradition." Florica looks at her husband with saucer-size eyes.

"Marrying young is not illegal," says Ivan, ignoring the reference to gypsy practices, which are now illegal in the Soviet Union.

The Sinti family begins playing, and Ivan Sawolynska loses his heart to Nadya. Ivan has spent his life moving up the ranks of the communist party and the governmental bureaucracy. He thinks it's time to settle down and start a family.

Ivan Sawolynska and Nadya Sinti marry. Ten months later, Nikolai Ivan Sawolynska is born. Nadya is overwhelmed with the baby, and Ivan finds a crying baby difficult. Nadya wants her parents, so Sasha and Nuri move in and help with the baby.

Ivan plays classical music and baby Nikolai quiets. Nadya and her parents play folk music and Nikolai quiets. Sasha tells Nikolai stories, and his favorite story is about a boy who falls asleep and wakes up to find he has turned into a whole note, but has the ability to change into a half note, a quarter note, an eighth, and finally into a sixteenth note. The note wakes up and finds he's a boy after all.

Nikolai has a gift to create new music. Ivan sends him to the Russian Academy of Music. Nikolai blends his classical training with his mother's and grandparents' traditional folk music. As an accomplished violinist, Nikolai joins the Moscow Symphony at the age of twenty-one. The conductor speaks of playing a few of his compositions. His father pulls strings, and Nikolai becomes a member of the Cultural Foundation.

A good friend, who works for the Bolshoi Orchestra, asks Nikolai to substitute for him while he attends to his sick mother in St. Petersburg. Nikolai agrees, and on his first day he falls in love with a ballerina with smooth complexion and large, dark eyes. Her name is Natalia Krasnov.

Nikolai and a few musicians overhear a conversation between Natalia and a tall, muscular, and tough-looking man. The musician next to Nikolai whispers, "He belongs to the Committee for State Security . . . the KGB. Peter Petrosky is his name. My advice to you is to be on his good side."

Nikolai talks to his father about the beautiful Natalia Krasnov and the menacing Peter Petrosky. Ivan can tell his son is in love. Ivan attends a meeting on how to handle the dissident situation outside of Moscow.

Peter Petrosky's name comes up as someone who could infiltrate the dissident group. They all agreed Peter is a good choice, and, if he is successful, it would enhance his career opportunities.

With Peter gone, Nikolai wins Natalia's heart. Natalia informs her mother, Irena Krasnov, who expresses a concern. "Are you sure you want to make an enemy of Peter Petrosky?"

Natalia shudders and her mind drifts into the distance. She mutters, "He's a brute. He scares me. I hope he stays away forever."

Irena knows men like Peter Petrosky because her father was like that. Irena expresses empathy for her daughter, but needs to be realistic. "Men with that kind of job are not forgiving types."

"Nikolai is kind. We're artists. We understand each other," says Natalia.

Natalia can't hide the desperation in her voice. "Perhaps Nikolai's father can help."

"Oh, Natalia, it's dangerous to be caught between powerful forces," says Irena, and yet she knows that is exactly where her daughter is headed.

When Peter Petrosky returns to Moscow and learns of the marriage, he is furious. He goes to the Bolshoi Ballet Company to confront Natalia, but she's on maternity leave. He then finds Natalia's mother, Irena, at the school where she coaches young singers. He waits until Irena is alone before he approaches her. His steely hazel-blue eyes burrow into her and he demands to know, "Why didn't you stop Natalia from marrying Nikolai Sawolynska?"

"Peter, please, I tried. I told Natalia you didn't abandon her. But your absence . . . you know how sensitive she is."

"You didn't try hard enough!"

"She is pregnant. Nikolai loves her enough to marry her."

Peter has fury in his eyes. "I will marry her. She must leave Nikolai."

"Nikolai puts Natalia first; can you?"

Peter knows he can't. "I will not allow another man to raise my child."

"Peter, if you truly love Natalia, you'll let her go."

"I'm a patient man. If it takes until the end of my days, I will make things right." Peter turns away from Irena and storms out.

Irena melts into her chair. Peter's intimidating style brings memories of her father. But she's not a child; she's an accomplished singer who has an affinity for opera. She told a small lie to keep Natalia safe. Then she grimaces, remembering lies in opera are used to thicken the plot.

Irena Krasnov decides her daughter's suggestion is worth pursuing and pays Ivan Sawolynska a visit. "Ivan, Peter Petrosky is angry about the marriage. He said that he is a patient man and if it takes to the end of his days, he will make things right. I am scared."

"Irena, it's good that you tell me this. Let me see what I can do."

Going home, Irena hopes her instigation won't return to bite her.

Ivan Sawolynska visits a friend in the Committee for State Security. They discuss the civic unrest outside of Moscow. Ivan casually comments on how well the last civil-unrest situation went. His friend's thought went exactly where Ivan had hoped and Peter Petrosky was dispatched to handle the crisis.

Peter returns to Moscow after finishing his assignment. He goes to the Bolshoi Ballet Company and waits in Natalia's dressing room, which she shares with other ballerinas. Peter motions everyone out except for Natalia.

"Hello, Natalia, you are as beautiful as ever."

"Peter, why are you here?"

"Is this any way to greet the father of your child?"

Taken aback, Natalia must wait for more information. Peter accommodates. "Your mother told me about the pregnancy and how the understanding Nikolai came to your aid. Do you have a picture of my child? Is it a boy or a girl?"

Natalia takes out a photo from her purse. Peter looks at a small child dressed in gypsy clothes with her hands extended out. He scrutinizes the girl for any resemblance to himself. Dark hair is the only thing he sees. Finally, he asks, "What she is doing?"

"Her name is Helena, and she is portraying Carmen."

"Is she any good?"

"Yes. Helena is a child prodigy. She loves opera and Carmen in particular."

"She gets her talent from your side since your mother sings. I would like to meet her," says Peter.

"That would not be a good idea."

"Why not?"

Natalia blows air out of her mouth and admits. "Helena is not your child. Our baby died in my womb. Nikolai is Helena's father."

"Oh, Natalia, I am so sorry." Peter silently gets up and leaves.

Helena Sawolynska's story is circulated among the artist community as a warning to cooperate. The Soviet audiences know Helena's story by heart. Her parents, Nikolai and Natalia Sawolynska, accomplished artists, died in a mysterious car accident when Helena was seven years old. Her great-grandparents, the Sintis, died when she was eight. Her grandfather Ivan Sawolynska died when she was nine. Her grandmother Nadya Sawolynska passed away when she was twelve. Helena's only living relative is her grandmother Irena Krasnov, the noted opera singer and current business manager of the Bolshoi Opera Company.

The newspaper lists the credits of Helena Sawolynska, which include leading roles in *Aida*, *Turandot*, *La Gioconda*, *Tosca*, and *Carmen*, on the great operatic stages within the Soviet Union. At the age of nineteen, offers from London, Paris, Sydney, New York, Los Angeles, and Tokyo arrive. It is said that her pure tones penetrate and move audience to places beyond words and that she sings like an angel.

In the fall of 1987, the Bolshoi Opera Company is granted permission by the Soviet government to begin an international tour starting in Tokyo, Japan. Performances sell out within minutes of availability in Japan. The Japanese newspaper gives Helena outstanding reviews, and ticket sales go through the roof in Sydney, Los Angeles, New York City, London, Paris, and Milan. One Japanese critic writes, "Ms. Sawolynska reaches into the depths and crevices of our emotional vulnerabilities with her vocal agility."

Irena returns to her makeshift office to find Peter Petrosky waiting for her. His deep-black hair has streaks of gray in it. Why does he keep popping up in her life?

"Hello, Irena. I could have saved Natalia had she married me."

"We cannot change the past," says Irena. "Must the KGB pressure artists?"

"Intimidation works. You can't believe the number of complying artists after the deaths of Natalia and Nikolai."

"How can you live with yourself?"

"I'm a pragmatist," replies Peter. "I am on tour with your company."

"Aren't you too high up for such a menial job?"

"If it weren't for me, your company wouldn't be allowed out of the Soviet Union. Besides, I deserve to see the fruits of my investment."

A guilty Irena remains silent.

When the Bolshoi Opera Company arrives in Australia, Katrina Adams and her assistant, Anya Lukin of the public relations department of the Sydney Opera House, greet Irena Krasnov, the manager of the Bolshoi Opera Company. "If you need anything, day or night, you just call," Katrina says and hands her their business cards. Irena thanks them and indicates she speaks a bit of English.

Irena enters Helena's dressing room. "The tour is going so well. You are capturing the world's heart just like I knew you would, sweet girl."

"When I sing, I'm free." Helena, with a mix of exuberance and hesitancy, informs her grandmother that

Peter Petrosky has invited her to dine with him. Helena lowers her voice and whispers, "He frightens me. I overhear he is KGB and recruits artists to be spies."

Irena winces as she delivers a dose of reality to her granddaughter. "As artists, we walk a fine line."

"But you know better than me that treachery and intrigue in opera never end well."

"Tell Peter Petrosky that I'll be going to dinner with you. Let's talk about something else."

With a sparkle in her eyes, Helena says, "I can't believe Great-Grandmama Sasha's vision is happening!" As a child, Great-Grandmama Sinti had told her stories of singing on stages around the world.

Irena pleads with her granddaughter in a gentle whisper. "It's not safe to share such things. Let me go and find a nice, quiet place for us to eat."

Irena goes to the Public Relations Office and asks Anya Lukin about a good place to go for dinner. Anya asks if she and Helena would be interested in having supper with her family tonight. Irena replies yes. Anya gathers Irena and Helena and ushers them to her car. Driving to her family home, Anya says, "I'm sure I'm breaking protocol for stealing the two of you away, but I've decided it is better to ask for forgiveness than to ask for permission. My parents are so honored to have you come to our home."

There is worry in Helena's voice. "I hope you won't be in too much trouble."

"To have this piece of quiet is most welcome and needed," replies Irena.

"That's exactly what I thought," says Anya.

Anya's parents prepared a Russian meal to make Helena and Irena feel at home. Over *vinegret*, a medley with pieces of herring, chopped beets, cucumber, carrot, potato, and oil, Irena and Helena learn of how the Lukins were able to find their way to freedom. Helena asks, "Weren't you scared to leave Russia?"

"It was worse to stay," say Anya's father.

Helena's skin color goes pale. Anya changes the topic. "We are so happy that you have come to Australia. Trina and I have been reading all the wonderful reviews from Japan. *Carmen* is my most favorite opera!"

With the serving of the traditional borscht soup and then the beef stroganoff, there is silence at the table. Everyone is savoring the meal.

Helena sips the *kvass* drink. "This is so good!"

"My father loves making it," laughs Anya.

"So simple! Water, flour and liquid malt and add a bit of flavor with raspberry or lemon. But for this one I used ginger and mint," says Anya's father.

"I see freedom agrees with you," says Irena.

"Yes, to be free is worth the cost of whatever price must be paid."

Irena sees fear in Helena's face. Irena is uncertain if it is for the cost of freedom or if it's for her grandmother's interest in it. Irena gives a pragmatic look to reassure her granddaughter.

Peter Petrosky storms into Irena's room, so Anya waits quietly outside the door.

"Where you were last night? I thought we could dine together. You can't wander the streets of Sydney alone. There are degenerates out there! People who dye their hair blue and green and have tattoos on their bodies."

"We had dinner at the home of a staff member. She wanted to go over press releases," says Irena. "I saw no harm. We were back at the hotel by 9 o'clock."

"You saw no harm! Helena is a Russian national treasure. She could have been kidnapped!" shouts Peter.

"But we're here and we're safe."

"It is not your job to think," shouts Peter. "That's my job! I'll tell you where you can go. From now on, you need my permission. Do you understand? Am I clear enough for you?"

"Yes," reply Irena and Helena in small voices.

"Good. Tonight, we'll go to dinner and talk about how you might get back on my good side. Helena, there is a diplomatic reception in your honor. I could use your help," says Peter in a suggestive tone.

Anya hears no response from Helena and moves quickly and quietly from the door. She returns when Peter leaves and notices how pale Helena and Irena are. Anya asks, "Is there anything more I can do for you?"

Irena takes Anya's hands and says, "You are a kind person. Thank you for a wonderful dinner last night."

"Will your parents be at the performance tonight?" asks Helena. Anya nods in the affirmative. Irena suggests they come backstage, but Anya hesitates. Her parents would be honored, but uncomfortable with the watchful eyes around. Irena understands, as her stomach turns a bit queasy.

The opening night performance is a huge success, with standing ovations and a plethora of flowers. Irena smiles as if it were she standing on the stage receiving the accolades.

Peter Petrosky watches everyone who comes to see Helena, like a guard. Peter congratulates Helena and

Irena. "Good job! I was talking with our ambassador and he wonders if you would be so kind as to sing a few songs for the party?"

Helena nods yes. "I'll give you a list of people to pay special attention to," says Peter, as Trina and Anya enter the room carrying two huge bouquets of flowers. Peter turns around and says, "How can two women walk so quietly?"

Anya and Trina are offended by Peter's comment. Anya stays silent, while Trina gets feisty. "I guess Australian women are much lighter on their feet than Russian women." Then Trina points to her shoes, "Hush Puppies. You might want to buy a pair while you're in Australia."

Peter laughs, but tension remains in his jaws. He sizes Anya up; she has no spunk with her mousy brown hair and inert green eyes. He puts his full attention on Trina. She is about five feet seven inches tall. With high heels on, he would still have the height advantage. Normally, he thinks women with blond hair don't possess much wit, but he notices her hazel eyes take in a lot and give away little. She is smarter than she appears.

With a smile, Trina hands a huge bouquet of flowers to Helena. "The Sydney Opera House is thrilled. We are sold out! Is there any way we can add any matinee performances?"

It is clear the question is really for Irena, who looks at Peter before responding. "I think so, but let me work it out on paper first."

"Tomorrow the artistic director and the contract person, both women, will talk with you," says Trina. Then she turns to Peter. "Would you like me to tell them to walk loudly or come in high heels?"

"Western women must give their men big headaches."

"And lots of happy grins, too," winks Trina and turns to Helena. "Thank you for a glorious opening night."

Peter Petrosky takes Helena and Irena to a family barbecue place for dinner. He orders for them, plus a pitcher of beer. They sit in quiet corner. Peter goes into great detail about what is required of them. It's clear they are to gather certain information for him.

Peter drinks the entire pitcher of beer and becomes talkative. "Irena, I never understood why you felt it necessary to lie to me and make me believe that Helena was my child. Why couldn't you tell me that Natalia lost my baby?" Peter turns to Helena. "Did you know you might have had an older sister or brother?"

Helena shakes her head no. She is confused by the conversation. To her, Peter's tone turns from menacing to morose. She feels scared, not just for herself, but for her grandmother, too. He seems to be playing cat and mouse with them.

Irena sees Helena's reaction of fear and tries to dissipate the topic by coming clean. She answers, "We were young and too emotional."

"I loved Natalia and I was angry at losing her. No one compared to her." He looks at Helena. "I felt horrible when I heard your mother had died. Even though I had nothing to do with your parents' death, I felt responsible. So out of love for your mother, I paid for your musical training and schooling, and now I have offered myself to be the security agent on this tour."

Helena gasps at this piece of information and turns to grandmother. Irena's eyes do not deny Peter's words. Peter says, "Irena, do you remember when I said I would make things right?"

Irena remembers all too well. She knows to stay quiet and just listen when a man drinks. "Well," says Peter, "that's what I have been doing. Tomorrow night you can show your gratitude." Peter had delivered his point: it's time to pay up.

When they return to the hotel, Helena and Irena go to bed. Helena hears her grandmother tossing and turning. Finally, she falls asleep. In her dream, Peter Petrosky is running her parents off the road. She wakes up with tears streaming down her face. She cries, but no sounds come out.

Irena can't sleep, so she checks on Helena. She finds her granddaughter in a distressed state and voiceless. It's early, but Irena locates Anya's business card and calls her. "Anya, Helena has no voice!"

Anya calms Irena down by saying that her boss, Trina Adams, is a very good problem solver and promises to call her back with a solution. Irena believes Anya; she hopes Anya will call back before Peter Petrosky shows up. She jumps when she hears a knock on the door. Irena cautiously goes to the door and asks, "Who is it?"

"Peter Petrosky, wishing you a good morning!" Irena wants to faint, but she doesn't. She opens the door to a Peter Petrosky grinning from ear to ear.

Peter sees the dark circles under Irena's eyes and asks, "Are you all right?" He looks around and asks, "Is Helena all right?"

Weary, Irena sighs. She starts to explain when the phone rings. She answers and listens carefully to what Anya is telling her. "I understand. Peter Petrosky has just arrived. Thank you." Irena hangs up the phone and turns to Peter to explain. "Helena woke up this morning with no voice. Trina Adams is on her way. Her sister is a doctor and Trina has managed to get an appointment for Helena this morning."

Anya informs Trina that Peter Petrosky is in the hotel room with Irena and Helena. Anya feels quite certain that Helena's voice loss is due to Peter Petrosky's threats. Anya expresses in an agitated voice that it is a well-known fact that Russian artists are pressured to gather information for the KGB. Trina rolls her eyes and lets out, "What a mess!"

While waiting for Trina, Peter scrutinizes Irena. "Why did you call Trina for help? Why didn't you call me?" Helena sits on the sofa like a stone statue. Irena looks at her granddaughter. "Look at her. She's not well. You're not a doctor. How can you help? Look at how quickly Trina managed the situation."

"Are you sure there is not more going on?" Peter burrows his eyes into Irena.

"What do you mean?" Irena asks in her most innocent tone.

"You play coy and helpless, but I know you are a cunning woman. You didn't blink an eye trying to pass Helena off as my daughter, but what if she is?" suggests Peter. "Maybe Natalia lied about our baby dying to protect Nikolai. Well, there is a new DNA procedure that allows scientists to cut out the unique sections of the DNA, which is extracted from blood samples. Since we are here, why not find out for sure."

Irena wants to scream at Peter. Why is he only thinking about himself? She wants to shove that DNA procedure up his . . . where the sun doesn't shine. She calms herself and waits for Trina. Trina arrives to take Helena to see her sister. Peter sits in the front seat and Trina can't resist playing with him. "Is it all right with you if I take Helena to see my sister?"

"Well, thank you for asking. It is better than someone from your staff taking her without getting my permission!" shouts Peter.

"In my country, we call this hospitality! We are friendly people. Kindness isn't against the law in the Soviet Union, is it?"

"Sarcasm is unbecoming, Ms. Adams. I'm just doing my job," replies Peter.

Trina turns into the Louise Parker Children's Research Center and Peter Petrosky reads the sign. "This is a place for children!"

"My sister is a respected pediatrician."

Trina leads the group to a waiting area outside her sister's office. They are informed that Dr. Adams is finishing up a conference call with a doctor from the United States. Peter asks Trina, "This is a research center, so they do scientific studies such things as DNA analysis?"

Trina gives Peter a weird look, "They study children's intuition. You might be a bit old to be tested, but do you want me to ask?"

"No!"

Peter Petrosky's strange questions and antiquated ways are getting on Trina's nerves. She decides she can't wait any longer and inches up to her sister's office door and then makes a quick entrance into her sister's office.

Trina notes the stunned look on her sister's face. "Eviann, you have to help me out of this soap opera! In the waiting room is Helena Sawolynska, the famous Russian opera singer who currently has no voice, her scared grandmother, and a chauvinistic KGB agent inquiring about DNA testing."

"Trina, I'm a pediatrician, not a psychologist or playwright," answers Eviann.

"This sounds exciting, like the James Bond novel, *From Russia with Love*. You know, Ian Fleming was in the British Foreign Intelligence Service—MI 6, I believe. Let's put on our espionage hats and help," says Angelica over the speaker phone.

"Angelica, this is my sister, Trina," says Eviann.

"Hi," says Trina, "I've heard a lot about you."

"Should we move toward solving your dire situation?" inquires Angelica.

"I like her," whispers Trina to Eviann.

"Eviann," says Angelica, "will you ask Great Uncle Ambrose to examine Helena, the grandmother, and the KGB agent?"

"Irena Krasnov and Peter Petrosky." Trina fills in the names.

Eviann peeks out through the mini blinds and makes her report. "Both women are dark pink. The KGB agent seems fine."

"That is so wrong on so many levels, but accurate," cries out Trina. "According to my assistant, Anya, he is a cat playing with a bird. She overheard him threatening them."

"It's emotional then," says Angelica.

Eviann asks, "Angelica, what do you recommend?"

"I would say anything to strengthen the immune system like garlic, carrots, ginger, spinach, turmeric, black pepper. A tincture of herbs for the bath might be helpful," replies Angelica. "Eviann, I think Helena might be one of us. I read about her. I think we need to make a space for her and see what happens."

Eviann opens the door and motions the group into her office. Peter Petrosky takes over and everyone is confused when he turns the subject to scientific DNA tests.

"Mr. Petrosky, do you believe Helena's voice loss is tied to her genetics?"

"Who is asking this question?" Peter looks around the office.

"I'm sorry, Mr. Petrosky, but I'm Dr. Angelica Mee. Dr. Adams and I were in conference when this emergency arose. I'm Dr. Adams's colleague and I am familiar with genetics, but more with plants than with people. But I have contacts and affiliations with many research centers around the world and some of them do DNA research." Dr. Mee answers from the speaker phone.

Peter looks at Eviann. "Can this center do DNA testing?"

"No," answers Angelica. "I have contacts in Los Angeles. I believe you'll be there during your tour."

"What can you do for Helena?" asks Irena.

"I'll need to examine her first," replies Eviann.

"I'll translate for you," says Peter.

"Eviann," says Angelica, "I speak Russian."

"Thank you, Mr. Petrosky, but Helena will be in the hands of not one, but two very good doctors." Eviann ushers everyone out of her office and asks the receptionist to transfer her call to examine room 1. The two ladies follow Eviann, much to the dismay of Peter Petrosky. Trina engages him, all the while thinking they don't pay her enough.

While Eviann takes Helena's blood pressure, Irena seizes on the opportunity to explain why Peter Petrosky wants the DNA tests. She adds to the story by saying she believes (along with the Russian artist community) that

Peter Petrosky is responsible for the death of her daughter and son-in-law. The only reason she and Helena are alive is because she told Peter that Helena was his child. That lie was her desperate attempt to save her family, even though it was not the truth. With pleading eyes, Irena asks if there is any way the test results could be altered to say he is the father.

Helena finally speaks, "I dreamed that he ran my parents off the road."

The two doctors understand immediately why Helena has lost her voice. Angelica explains in Russian that she has contacts in London, England, to help them seek asylum and asks if that is what she and her granddaughter want. Irena, remembering Anya's father's words about the high price of freedom, answers yes. Helena issues a nervous smile, but color returns to her face when she says, "Yes."

Helena asks, "Can you say that I cannot sing tonight at the party because I need to rest my voice and not speak?"

Dr. Eviann Adams smiles and replies, "Helena Sawolynska, I order you to rest your voice. Use it only for the performance tonight."

After further thought, Angelica gives specific instructions that tinctures of chamomile, sage, and skullcap be given and explains that these are remedies for calming nerves. Irena asks if she might have some, too.

That night, Helena sings and once again receives a long standing ovation. Helena and Irena attend the party in honor of the Bolshoi Opera Company, but everyone knows that the guests have come to see Helena Sawolynska. The host has been informed that Ms. Sawolynska must rest her voice. The guests can meet her, but not engage her in conversation. The diplomat is disappointed, but he can see for himself that Ms. Sawolynska is pale. Peter Petrosky spends the evening observing Helena and Irena.

The two women request to leave the party, and Peter taunts, "So early!" But the Russian diplomat intervenes, "Peter, Helena did Russia proud. Let them go, but you, my comrade, must stay so we can catch up."

In Los Angeles, Helena is accompanied by Irena and Peter to see Dr. Angelica Mee. "You are Chinese. I didn't know if that was your married name," says Peter.

"Mee is my maiden name," responds Angelica.

"Oh, John Ming Mee is your father. Interesting how he and his mentor left China and emigrated to England." Peter gives a smug look.

Angelica ignores Peter Petrosky's feign tactics and, in light and joyful tones, she says, "I am honored that you have gone out of your way to know my family history. Are you ready for the DNA test?"

"Yes, but how do you know how to speak Russian?"

Angelica prepares Peter's arm to draw blood. "When I was young, I had a Russian friend."

"Test Helena, too," says Peter. Angelica takes blood from Helena and Irena and Peter asks why.

Angelica kindly explains. "Helena's mother is not here, but her grandmother is. Half of Helena's mother's genetic makeup comes from Irena."

"You are very competent and you don't miss much." Peter speaks with a tone of admiration.

"I didn't get away with much growing up with two observant parents," laughs Angelica. Finally, she asks Peter Petrosky what he hopes to find out from the DNA tests.

He explains that Natalia was pregnant with his child when she married Nikolai Sawolynska, at least that is what Irena told him, but he confronted Natalia and she said their baby died. He wants to know the truth. Angelica conveys that if she had known his intention earlier, a paternity test could have been performed Sydney. He asks how soon before the results will be available. Angelica asks for addresses for him in New York and London because it will be a while, since this is not an emergency and the lab is backed up.

Angelica detects a slight sigh of relief from Irena. Angelica takes this opportunity to examine Helena privately. Irena asks if she could examine her too. Irena and Helena leave with more herbal remedies and with the knowledge that arrangements have been made in London. In return, Irena gives two tickets for Angelica and her husband, Pablo, to attend the evening performance of *Carmen*.

That evening Peter Petrosky sits next to Angelica Mee and Pablo Mora. Angelica introduces her husband, to which Peter responds, "Dr. Mee, you are very modern. You don't take your husband's name."

"Or I'm very old-fashioned and I prefer to keep my surname and not take hers," replies Pablo.

Angelica smiles, "Isn't it always a matter of perspective?"

"Perhaps," says Peter and then leans in. "Your family is good friends with Sir Laurence Edward, who has a foundation dedicated to helping artists and scientists to adjust to the West. You know defection is frowned upon in my country. We wouldn't want to think arrangements could be made over a few herbal remedies."

"From what I hear," says Pablo, "there is a lot that is frowned upon in your country. Thank goodness I live in this country and not in yours."

"But your wife has dual citizenship, US and British, does she not?" Peter sneers.

"And she is my wife in both countries. I'm a very lucky man," replies Pablo.

Angelica shrugs her shoulders and gives Peter a helpless look. Pablo takes her hand and she leans toward him and places her head on his shoulder.

In New York, Tatiana Trotsky, the understudy to Helena Sawolynska, approaches Peter Petrosky. "Mr. Petrosky, why don't you invite me to dine with you?"

"How about tonight, Ms. Trotsky?"

Peter takes her to a nice family Italian restaurant. Over dinner, Tatiana explains to him, "I was the rising star until Helena Sawolynska came along. She is so young. I don't know how I can get my chance. Can you advise me?"

"What is it that you think I can do?"

"You know how things work. Are there things I can do? I know sometimes I get tired and then I put on a bit of weight. I heard in Australia that Helena went to doctors that helped her to regain her voice and to keep up her energy. Perhaps, you can help me like that," smiles Tatiana.

"Let me see what I can do."

While he waits for the results of the DNA tests, he asks around for a good herbalist. The herbalist gives him a mixture of licorice, ginseng, and ephedra and another mixture with guarana for keeping one's energy up. Peter is pleased to deliver these remedies to Tatiana. She is elated at his help and attention.

When Irena and Helena leave their hotel room, Tatiana sneaks and switches out the herbal remedies. Tatiana watches Helena and Irena for behavioral changes. Irena's heart flutters the day before leaving for London. She is taken to the emergency room and then admitted to the hospital. The doctors forbid her to fly; more tests are needed. Blood results show Irena has too many stimulants in her system. They ask her what she is taking. She tells them to call Dr. Angelica Mee. When Angelica learns about the stimulants, she realizes Irena Krasnov is in danger and convinces her to defect to the British Embassy immediately. Nothing will be issued publicly until Helena is secured in London.

When the Bolshoi Opera Company arrives in London's famed Covent Gardens, Peter Petrosky is beside himself when he learns Irena is still in New York. He goes to the office to call the Russian Embassy, when he is informed that he has a call from Dr. Angelica Mee. He takes the call, hoping that Angelica can provide the information about Irena. Instead, he learns that Angelica is in London with the DNA results. She is doing a site consultation. Could he meet her this afternoon at an Italian restaurant across from St. Paul's Church? He agrees to the meeting.

Peter seeks out Helena to find out what she knows about her grandmother. Helena breaks down and cries, saying Irena is very sick. Peter tries to reassure her by placing his hand on Helena's back to comfort her, but her body is literally shaking. He quietly utters, "Don't worry. I'll take care of you." There is a knock on the door and a voice announces, "Sound check." Helena pulls herself together by taking a gulp of her herbal tonic.

Peter watches Helena until she is safely on stage and then leaves to meet Angelica. As Helena begins to sing for a sound check, her heart beats fast. She feels weird and passes out. She can't be revived. While the staff is calling the paramedics, the Queen's secretary is on another line, calling to say the Queen is unable to attend the evening's performance due to a cold. When the Queen hears of Helena's condition, she sends her personal physician straightaway to meet Helena at the hospital. The Queen's physician calls Sir Laurence Edward's residence, and his grandson, William Edward, is sent to assist Helena Sawolynska with her defection.

One of the paramedics goes to Helena's dressing room and grabs all the tinctures, as a manner of protocol. It is always good to know what is in the person's bloodstream, as there may have been something strange in the tinctures.

Dr. Angelica Mee and Peter Petrosky sit across from each other at the restaurant. She opens the envelope and pulls out the report. She takes a deep breath before launching into the report. "The results are unexpected and deserve an explanation in person."

Peter asks Angelica not to be polite, but rather to be direct and asks, "Am I Helena's father or not?"

Angelica picks her words carefully. "You have more genetic matches with Irena than you do with Helena. In fact, the report indicates that you and Irena most likely share the same father."

"That can't be! Did the lab mix up the samples?" Peter becomes solemn and memories flood in. His father never liked him. His mother protected him the best she could. Now he knows why. "Does Irena know?"

"Do you want her to know?" Angelica asks Peter.

Peter thinks a moment. "Irena is my half sister; Natalia, my niece; and Helena, my great niece. So it is good that Natalia and I never married?"

"Genetically wise, yes," answers Dr. Mee. "I hope you understand why I wanted to explain this report to you in person."

"Why are you so kind?"

"I find love and kindness to be a more enjoyable way to live. Besides, fear and violence have a mighty grip on this planet we call Earth." Angelica smiles sweetly at Peter.

"And I am good with fear and violence," admits Peter. "So tell me, is helping Helena and Irena defect a loving thing to do?"

"My family and I have dedicated our lives to being servants, instruments of joy. Children intuitively know how to be playful and joyful. If children could be nurtured from the beginning, how different would this world be? Could I interest you in joining our cause?"

"You're an idealist."

"Many would agree with you. I confess I'm a dreamer. But it always begins with a dream. Look around you. Everything you see someone has envisioned before they created it. Imagination is the first step. I envision and I believe in a different world, where children's gifts are identified and nurtured from the beginning."

"I believe you because you took the time to meet with me. I don't know that I would have done the same," says Peter.

"I felt I owed it to you. We are all travelers and we all deserve compassion. Can you not extend that kindness to Helena and Irena?"

"Have you taken Irena already?" asks Peter.

Angelica answers with a question, "Peter, did you try to hurt Irena?"

"Why would you say that?"

"Because Irena was given licorice, gingseng, ephedra, and guarana, which caused her heart to speed up," answers Angelica.

Peter realizes what happened. He tells Angelica that Tatiana asked for the formula to keep her weight down and energy up. He is certain it was jealousy that drove Tatiana to switch the remedies.

"Peter, what will you do?"

Peter assures Angelica that he will figure out a way that will work for everyone. Angelica believes him and offers her services should he require them in the future. Peter tells her the world is certainly a better place because she is in it.

By the time Peter returns to the theater, paramedics have taken Helena to the hospital. She wakes up and requests asylum. She learns her grandmother is on her way to London. An arrangement has been made for the two of them to stay in London, provided by the Laurence Edward Foundation.

The British government is astounded when they find that the Russian government has downplayed the two defections. The agent in charge convinces the Russian establishment that having Tatiana Trotsky in their pocket is worth more than the embarrassment of revealing the understudy's effort to maim the star and her grandmother.

It will be well into the new year of 1990 before Helena Sawolynska might return to the world stage. Meanwhile, she is learning English from Sir Laurence Edward's grandson, William. They become close friends.

During the holidays, William takes Helena to a small, cozy café to listen to Rajko play his violin. Rajko and his violin are one. His music is passionate. Between sets, Rajko comes over to greet William, who introduces Helena Sawolynska.

"Ms. Sawolynska, when I told my great-grandmother that you were coming tonight, she insisted that I bring you over to the house. She has a message from your family. Will you come?" Helena nods yes.

Rajko, William, and Helena enter a dimly lit room. They hear the woman's voice before they see her. A tall, slender woman emerges from a lounge chair and moves well for her age. She pats the dining room table, inviting them to sit. Rajko kisses his grandmother and excuses himself, leaving Helena and William in her care.

"I am Sophia. A long time ago, I did a reading for two women who are on the other side. I knew them as Sasha and Nadya Sinti."

Helena covered her mouth. "My grandmamma and great-grandmamma."

"They want me to do a tarot reading for you." She holds a bundle wrapped in silk and requests that what is most needed by the soul be revealed. She uncovers the cards and spreads them out in front of Helena.

Helena slides her hand across the cards and points to two cards. Sophia explains, "This card is a lineage card. *Le Mat* or *Le Fou*, the Fool who goes on the supreme adventure—to the gates of divine wisdom. The Fool is strong enough to travel across centuries. Your grandmother picked the same card."

Helena's grin widens. "I know they are here. I can feel them."

Sophia laughs and explains the second card. "This is another lineage card. *Le Chariot*, the Chariot.

"Grandmama chose this card too."

Sophia nods yes. "It is the vibration of your blood-line. You belong to a group of people who have guarded sacred ideas and have been waiting for the charioteer to cross the finish line."

"When I was very young, Great-Grandmama told me that I would be singing all over the world. How are the cards connected to this vision?" asks Helena.

"When you sing, you touch and move people. The energy creates an open space for forgotten ideas to come again. They believe you are the long-awaited chari-oteer." Sophia knows her work is almost done. "I'm told you've already met a few people committed to this new or forgotten principle." Helena knows it must be Dr. Mee and Dr. Adams.

Sophia concludes with the history of the tarot cards and of the Gypsy people. William can't believe it. He had just read about that in Manly P. Hall's book, *Secret Teaching of All Ages*. Sophia hands Helena the Fool and the Chariot cards for inspiration and to remind her that she travels on this path not alone but with her entire family line supporting her. As Helena receives the cards, she feels enchantment. Perhaps, it is the new or forgotten principle that Sophia has just mentioned. Whatever the reason, joy fills her heart and she feels content and at peace.

≈ 6 ≈

Ashlar Rachel Taylor: Making ART

The sunlight rises over the central Arizona desert. Archeologist Rachel Taylor is trekking through South Mountain Park, one of the largest municipal parks in the United States. She is striving to rid herself of an unconscious weariness in her bones. A cool, dry air hangs in the lower atmosphere this March morning, which indicates that this will be a warmer-than-average day. Her long, blond ponytail swings to and fro as she hikes. Her blue eyes take in the creosote bushes, which she sniffs for the scent of the desert.

With an unclouded mind, she drifts back to the winter's solstice at the Ramses II and Nefertari temples in Abu Simbel. Grandfather Taylor worked the Valley of the Kings site and had secured two tickets for her and Grandma Taylor. She was fifteen. She will never forget how she was captivated by the sunlight traveling through four courtyards and then reaching the inner recesses where four statues stood. She held her breath the entire time. Grandfather Taylor had explained the representation of the statues: the first three represented the physical, intellectual, and emotional aspects of man, and the last, headless statue represented the primordial energy, where light never reaches.

Grandma Taylor shared a story about the fourth representation. "It was the hands of Hauhet and her brother that bring forth the cosmic egg, the God of Light, RA, out of water. I hope this helps you understand why sunlight stops after the third statue." It didn't really, but this Egyptian magical moment, gifted by Grandfather and Grandma Taylor, led Rachel to become an archeologist, and she would be drawn to folktales and mythology to help understand the cultures of the past.

It is this passion that led her to this Arizona desert.

Being in good physical shape, her five-foot-seven-inch body hardly notices the trail going up or the weariness of 'is that all there is?' emerging. To reassure herself, she reviews her accomplishments: graduated from Kamehameha High School at sixteen, master's degree in archeology at twenty-two, published at twenty-four, and now project director of the La Villa project, the largest known Hohokam Village in the Phoenix area.

With the sun rising higher in the sky, she spots petroglyphs. Her child self smiles and she muses aloud, "Tell me your stories."

A voice out of nowhere shouts, "Only if you tell me your story first."

A startled Rachel Taylor reacts. "When I was a child, rocks never made demands. How times have changed!"

A petite woman with glistening black hair and almond-shaped eyes steps into the open. "It's the nature of rocks to drive a hard bargain. But I'm human with a soft touch. Hello, I'm Angelica Isatis Mee, and it is I who ask for your story."

Archeologist Taylor sees a woman filled with radiance. She responds professionally. "You're wise indeed; it's far easier to get my story than the story behind the rock, since no one knows for certain what these drawings mean—we can only speculate. It's a pleasure to meet you. I'm Ashlar Rachel Taylor, but I go by Rachel."

"Interesting. I think only a person with such an unusual first name would ask unanswerable questions."

Rachel explains that Ashlar is an Egyptian masonry word that means a squared stone, but more of a symbol for a material that has been worked upon as a result of creative activity. Her Swedish grandmother Rachel studied the mysteries of life and named her daughter Ashlar when she discovered the word in the symbol's dictionary. "My parents named me after the Swedish women on my father's side because I resemble them."

"Ashlar is a symbol for every human child," says Angelica. "You must have heard wonderful Swedish folktales."

Rachel nods in the affirmative. "I heard Norse tales from Grandma Ashlar and Hawaiian stories from Tutu, I mean grandmother, Alana. My 'Anake, auntie, Pauline accompanied my siblings and me each summer . . . " A surge of unexpected emotion bubbles up and Rachel can't go on.

Angelica waits a moment before coming to Rachel's rescue. "It's me. My husband calls me a walking truth serum. In truth, I am just a receptive vessel. Something in you wants out." Rachel's distant face guides Angelica to tell a story. "Not too long ago, a teenager swore that she had a foolproof method of creating a good porn-star name."

Captivated, Rachel asks, "I'll bite. How do I get one?"

"It is easy. You take the name of your first pet and your mother's maiden name. So, my porn name is Peppermint Lee. The young girl gave me two thumbs up."

Rachel smiles and says, "Leho Kalapana. That doesn't roll off the tongue like Peppermint Lee."

"But certainly more exotic," says Angelica.

"Exotic dancing would be an interesting culture to study. Yikes, that's my problem—too many interests and so little time. I will be working on the site of the largest documented Hohokam village," says Rachel.

Angelica's eyes light up. She pulls a business card out of her pocket and hands it to Rachel. "Miriam Whitefoot works at the Marcum G. Garver Foundation and Research Center. Miriam knows elders, the descendants of the ancient people who once lived around here. Maybe she can introduce you to an elder who knows a few sacred, healing stories. Open your heart and listen. Doorways will open."

Rachel looks at the card in awe. "Thank you for this contact!"

Smiling, Angelica says, "I have lived among several indigenous cultures, and selecting a name is done with much thought and care. Did you notice that both of our names spell out a word? My name spells AIM and yours spells out ART." Angelica glances at her watch and turns a final observation into a challenge. "Remember, Leho Kalapana, your restlessness brought you here today. I hope the next time we meet you will be living ART, getting at the heart of the matter and not just digging in the dirt, analyzing facts of what people of the past have left behind."

Angelica heads down the path and disappears. In disbelief at what has just transpired, Rachel holds the business card in her hand like a touchstone. She wishes she could contact Miriam Whitefoot immediately, but her new project requires her undivided attention.

The temperatures are already in the low 90s when the La Villa project begins. Those high double-digit temperatures in March turn into triple-digit temperatures in April and May. Rachel and the team's sweat glands go into overdrive and make the portable toilets hot and ripe. Rachel focuses on her love of surveying and mapping the site. She must document as much as possible within the contract time frame.

The backhoes arrive and she watches as each layer of soil is scraped away to reveal the levels of civilizations beneath the earth: the 1960s, the 1950s, 1940s, 1930s, 1920s, and further back. Long pin flags mark the features: pots, floors, postholes, hearths, and bottles from the 1920s.

Whole homes provide an opportunity to gather information about the day-to-day life of a prehistory culture. The hearth is placed near the entrance of the home. The hearth reveals the direction of the house and whether there is one home or multiple dwellings. The pit houses, extramural features, and concentrations of fire pits all indicate community gatherings where rites and stories must have been told and shared.

Rachel marvels at the cleverness of the ancient people. They used caliche, crusted calcium carbonate, to keep small critters out of their homes and to fireproof their walls. Extramural features might indicate village artists. Their granary and their canal systems indicate the ancient people were farmers. Time and time again, Rachel sees that ancient does not mean primitive. She thinks of the ancient people of Egypt, and she knows they are special and filled with hidden knowledge.

A tanned Rachel stands looking at the site. So many lives have been lived on this land. She can't get over how this ancient site is now a rundown part of Phoenix with a cemetery on one side and railroad tracks nearby. When the security fence around the site comes down, the land

and the people will change again. She must now convert the mounds of silent dirt and uncovered artifacts into graphs and information for other archeologists. Fortunately, this part of the project takes place in an air-conditioned office.

Rachel can now call Miriam Whitefoot. "You're the Hawaiian archeologist working on the old village site that Angelica told me about. I'll be going to the Salt River Reservation the next two weekends." They agree upon a date to meet at the front entrance of the Marcum G. Garver Foundation and Research Center at 6 A.M., Anglo time. Miriam asks Rachel if she needs directions.

Rachel says, "Is it off of Southern between McClintock and Rural and surrounded by a pond and some trees? Does Anglo time means 5:50 A.M.?"

Miriam laughs, "Excellent, you're bicultural!"

By 6 A.M., the ladies are traveling Country Club Drive heading toward Highway 87. Heading toward the reservation, Miriam explains to an eager Rachel, "Aunt Suzie is a Pima elder and healer. She rarely meets with outsiders. You must be special. I was told it is best to listen like an empty vessel. I have things to do, which should give you ample time to visit."

When they arrive at Aunt Suzie's place, Miriam makes introductions with a promise to return for a late lunch. Aunt Suzie heats up water and places the brewing teapot and two teacups on the table. "I understand you are working on the old village site. What have you found?"

"Some whole homes and plenty of potsherds," says Rachel.

"A potsherd," laughs Aunt Suzie. "There is a Pima legend about a potsherd. Anna Moore Shaw tells the story in her book *Pima Indian Legends*. Centuries ago, the Hohokam Indians lived in the fertile valleys along the Salt and Gila rivers. No one knows for sure why the people left. In their flight, an olla (a water jug) breaks and shatters into pieces. One piece cries to the elements, 'Remember my people.' The sand and wind cover the potsherd for safekeeping. Generations pass and the potsherd feels it is time to return. The wind blows the sand away and the rain washes the potsherd clean, allowing a Pima girl to find it. The girl falls in love with the pattern and inscription. She takes it home and copies them onto a new olla."

Rachel emerges from story trance while Aunt Suzie pours tea into two cups. Rachel remembers to listen with open heart or was it like an empty vessel? She dismisses the question and says, "How fabulous to have a story that links the lost people of the past with the Pimas of today!"

"Stories hold truth in plain sight, like the beautiful words written on a piece of potsherd. The listeners decide on the level of truth received. The women in my family are story keepers. Stories feed my spirit. Since I was a little girl, I have loved Grandmother Spider. Grandmother Spider and Coyote helped me through the American school system. Today, stories and I are a team. I provide the voice; they provide the spiritual vision." Aunt Suzie sips her tea. "Do you tell sacred stories?"

Rachel starts to say how much she loves folktales and mythology when she chokes up. She shakes it off and tells Aunt Suzie about her summers on the Forbidden Isles where the traditional Hawaiian ways of life are practiced. She describes living in a thatched hut. She describes gathering guava, coconut, and taro root. She speaks of making flower leis for special occasions and learning to hula and chant. When she shares how she used to sit knee to knee with her Hawaiian grandmother and recite special stories, Rachel stops talking because she can't go on.

"What happened?" asks Aunt Suzie.

Rachel pulls herself together and replies. "My siblings have Hawaiian names that roll off the tongue, beautiful olive complexions, and golden brown eyes. My younger sister, Leilani, teaches Hawaiian culture at the community college at home. My older brother, Kahu, is a lawyer and community activist. When I'm not tanned, I look more like the goddess Freya than like the goddess Pele or Hina."

Aunt Suzie acknowledges the hurt. "Rachel, I am a healer who travels to other realms looking for lost portions of one's soul. Darkness lies in our wounds of past hurts, not in the color of our skins. As I've told you, stories brought me home. And now it is my job to use stories to bring other people home."

Aunt Suzie's empathy relaxes Rachel enough for Aunt Suzie to share an observation. "Hawaiians and Native Americans have a lot in common." Then Aunt Suzie's eyes drift upwards. "I'm being told to invite you to two storytelling healing ceremonies that will be here on my property. They take place on the third and fourth weekend in October."

Rachel responds with delight, "I'm so honored."

"Good. Come Friday evening. I prepare with a cleansing ritual the night before. I think you'll find it interesting."

There is a knock on the door before the two women realize how much time has passed. Miriam suggests a local place for lunch, where she catches Aunt Suzie up on news outside of the reservation.

Because Rachel lives on the mainland, her family has established a custom for her to call home to Hawaii. They gather around the speakerphone so they can hear Rachel and she can hear them. This Sunday, she shares the news of meeting Aunt Suzie and the invitation to two Pima healing ceremonies.

"What an amazing opportunity!" says her father. "When you come home, you can be my expert guest in my undergraduate cultural anthropology classes. Of course, you will share that potsherd story."

"Rachel, honey," chimes her mother. "Did Aunt Suzie mention sharing matrilineal lines?"

"Yes, she did," answers Rachel.

"Rachel, this is Grandma Ashlar. Don't forget you come from a long line of powerful women. Did Aunt Suzie share any Grandmother Spider or Coyote stories?"

Rachel's paternal grandmother is a folklorist. "No, Gram, but she did say how important they were to her."

"Rachel, this is Auntie Pauline. I hope you listen like a *keiki*." Rachel notices the recurring message to listen with an open heart, like an empty vessel and now like a child. Her family informs her of upcoming events, so they won't be available for a while. Rachel hears chimes of aloha and then the hum of the dial tone.

Rachel and her colleagues see a notice about a storytelling festival in the Bradshaw Mountains. They decide to attend. In the morning, they hear folktales, myths, and personal stories. In the afternoon, they participate in a storytelling circle. Joseph Martens facilitates her group. He offers three story prompts: your name story, your favorite folktale, or why did you come to this festival? Joseph begins with a story. "I came to story through genealogy. Martens is a Danish name, so I researched Danish folktales and became enamored with gnomes. My good friend, Peggy Moroney, coined a new word for us: Nanology—the study of gnomes."

Martens patiently waits for someone to speak. "I'm Beauregard A Strickler. The A is just A. My parents couldn't decide between Ansel and Anderson. I'm afraid I'm scarred for life, left with an incomplete picture of myself. But my Australian schoolmates called me BoA Constrictor, alias the Snake, which I like."

Bo's story encourages Rachel to share her name story. "I'm Ashlar Rachel Taylor, which spells out ART. Ashlar is an Egyptian word that my Swedish great-grandmother found in the symbols dictionary. I've been told there is magic in stories if I listen like a child, and I am intrigued with the idea of story being a messenger. That's why I am here."

When the storytelling circles end, Rachel finds Bo standing next to her. "I'm interested in story magic, too. With your interesting background, you must be rich with stories." Rachel looks at Bo and thinks to herself that he doesn't even know the half of it. He asks her if she has seen the Bill Moyers series *Joseph Campbell and the Power of Myth*. He tells her it is filled mythology and folktales. Before she can escape him, he asks if he could hear more of her story.

Rachel wonders if a story can be a messenger, can people be messengers too? Then reality sets in and she answers responsibly. "I have a huge archeological report weighing on me at the moment." Bo shares that he is a civil engineer and understands the importance of her work. He has benefited from such reports. While she hesitates, he shoves his business card into her hand, which she slips into her purse.

Professor Chip O'Donnell, the chair of Rachel's master's thesis committee, and his wife invite her to their home for dinner. Mrs. O'Donnell prepares crusted salmon over a spring mix with balsamic vinaigrette. Over a glass of claret wine, the topic of Public Broadcasting System (PBS) and the recent showings of *Joseph Campbell and the Power of Myth* with Bill Moyers comes up.

"I swear, when Joseph Campbell tells a folktale, his eyes are radiant and words flow through him. Rachel, have you seen any of the series?" inquires Mrs. O'Donnell.

"No, but you're the second person to recommend it."

"Rachel, you must find time. Truly, I enter another realm of consciousness when I listen to the series, and it's been a gold mine for finding stories. I belong to a writing/journal group. This new guy wrote the most delightful story about his name. He has only a middle initial, which has ruined him for life," laughs Mrs. O'Donnell.

Rachel wonders if it could be. She locates her purse and pulls out Bo's business card. "His name isn't Bo A Strickler is it?"

"Oh, my, synchronicity at work!" shouts Mrs. O'Donnell.

Dr. O'Donnell chuckles. "I have learned not to mess with women's intuition. My wife believes this is a message for you."

Rachel laughs and suspects it's true.

As instructed, Rachel arrives at Auntie Suzie's home the evening before the event. Rachel follows Aunt Suzie to the sweat lodge. Aunt Suzie places a bundle in a holder on a pole and motions Rachel to sit. Aunt Suzie begins to chant. Rachel smells sage through the moist air and she drifts away. She is in a dark place, but she is not alone. She is with Grandma Ashlar at New Grange in Ireland. It is Winter's Light, a time where the veil between the two worlds of light and dark becomes transparent. A priestess performs the ritual to keep the discarnate spirits from possessing the living humans. The priestess is her Great-Grandma Rachel!

Rachel opens her eyes and hears the crackle of water over the hot rocks. Auntie Suzie asks, "What did you see?" Rachel shares her vision. Auntie Suzie replies, "Your eternal ancestors are speaking to you."

"Why?"

"I think that is for you to figure out."

"Can you give me a hint?"

"I find being an empty vessel and opening my heart fully before the ancestors to be helpful. I love hearing from them and I miss them when they are silent, unless they're all talking to me at the same time. I can't process it fast enough and I end up with a big, fat headache! I have to remind them that I'm stuck in this body, so one at a time, pleeaasse!"

Auntie Suzie's lightheartedness makes Rachel laugh. Auntie Suzie informs her, "We'll rise before the sun, greet the ancestors, and listen to whichever sacred, healing stories desire to be told. Then we'll have a light meal and wait for the people to arrive."

With the Red Mountains at Auntie Suzie's back, she holds the calendar stick with one hand while the other hand slides to the symbol of the story that wants to be told. The drums begin beating. The pulsating rhythm takes Rachel away. She senses Coyote's presence before she sees his two pointed ears, his yellow eyes, and his mangy fur and tail. Coyote calls forth an elderly woman with a pointy chin and big, hooked nose and dances with her. The woman changes into a salmon, a seal, and then a fly. Coyote motions someone else to come forth. It's Maui with his surf board. Maui looks around, shakes his head, and disappears. Coyote and the fly throw their hands up in disappointment.

Auntie Suzie asks Rachel. "What did you experience?" Rachel tells her about Coyote, the old woman who changes, and Maui. Aunt Suzie chuckles. Her eyes have a mischievous twinkle. "Trickster spirits are messengers. You must be one tough cookie!"

Rachel shakes her head in disbelief. Could Angelica, Aunt Suzie, her entire family, and now Mrs. O'Donnell have lined up like the Pony Express, waiting to intercept her? Thank goodness this weekend her family is home. Rachel calls and shares her experiences at the storytelling festival, her dinner with the professor and his wife, and her two visions with Aunt Suzie.

"Rachel, this is Grandma Ashlar. The changeling is Loki!"

"Rachel, this is Auntie Pauline. Tricksters . . . that is good!"

Rachel shouts, "But what does it mean?"

"Huna prayers, listen," advises her mother.

"Rachel, come home and we can see the *Joseph Campbell and the Power of Myth* series with Bill Moyers together. We can talk about the importance of tricksters," counsels Grandma Ashlar.

"Aaarrgggh! I've been told that three times! What is the message? What is dancing all around me?" howls Rachel.

"Rachel! Come home when your project is done," says her mother.

Surprised by her outburst, Rachel calms down. "I am sorry. I love you all."

In light, comfy clothes, Rachel leaves for Aunt Suzie's for the second sacred ceremony. As they enter the sweat lodge, Aunt Suzie pours water over the hot stones, and steam rises, releasing the scent of sage. Once they are seated across from each other, Aunt Suzie shuts her eyes, takes several deep breaths, and chants. The rhythmic sounds carry Rachel away. She hears people calling her name. She wants to go, but she can't. There is a barrier between her and them. She opens her eyes and asks Aunt Suzie, "What does this mean?"

With concern in her eyes, Aunt Suzie answers, "I think more will be revealed tomorrow."

The ceremony begins with Aunt Suzie calling the ancestors for healings for the people present. She slides her hands to the symbol on the calendar stick for the story to be told, and the rhythm of the drums beats out. Rachel goes within. She feels the eyes of the ancient ones shining through the mists. She sees the Norse seers, Druid priestesses, the Egyptian priestesses, the ancient Hawaiian ones, and her *aumakua* (family guides) standing before her in silence. They make a space for her.

Rachel weeps. Later, she asks Aunt Suzie, "Why do they want me?"

"Rachel, you won't know until you face the hurt that blocks you from knowing and seeing. It's up to you. Whatever you decide, you still owe me a Hawaiian story."

Rachel phones her family and shares her recent experiences with Aunt Suzie. Rachel prepares for an assault of comments from the women in her family, but they are silent.

"Rachel, how is the report coming along? When can I schedule you to talk to my classes?" asks her father.

"I'm almost done." Rachel hears clapping hands.

"This is Mom. I can't wait to see you!"

"But the company has asked me to hang around because they have two possible contracts coming up," answers Rachel.

"What! Are your ears full of wax?" screams Auntie Pauline.

"Rachel, you need your family's help. How many more messengers can we send?" says Grandma Ashlar.

"Rachel, this is your father. Come home and while you are here, you can consider a doctorate in anthropology."

"You mean you want me to come home for good, not just for a visit. Why didn't you folks say so before?" asks Rachel.

"We have!"

Rachel's defenses drop partially away. "Okay. I'll come home for at least a visit once the report is complete." She hears grumbling and a collective sigh.

At last Rachel arrives in Hawaii. Her family wraps her in flower leis. At the family compound, she receives a schedule. Puzzled, she asks, "What's this?"

"Auntie Pauline calls it family talk time," replies Grandma Ashlar.

"Trust us, honey," says her mother.

The family keeps her up until 9 P.M. so she can acclimate to local time.

The next morning, Rachel goes to the kitchen and meets with her father, who says, "Let's go to Kimo's for your favorite breakfast."

"Dad, just thinking about Hawaiian sweetbread with *lilikoi* butter syrup makes my mouth water."

Waiting for their order to be placed, Rachel's father shares how Auntie Pauline made them pull names out of a hat for the Rachel schedule and how he won first place. He tells her about the new doctorate program in anthropology at the university and hopes she will give it serious consideration. He reminds her that archeology has been good to the Taylor family. His eyes light up. "Here comes your brother. You're in luck for some good Taylor men advice."

Rachel meets with Grandma Ashlar next. They find a small grove of ironwood trees and nestle their chairs into the sand facing the ocean. They sit a while listening to the sounds of the Pacific Ocean and become mesmerized by the beautiful ocean colors of aquamarine green and ultramarine blue near the horizon.

"I sit here and before I know it, I regain my balance and answers come," says Grandma Ashlar. "Your grandfather and I took you to Egypt because, ever since you were young, the ancient ones have known you." Grandma Ashlar laughs and says, "The ancient ones have turned you into an archeological site, using the ethereal backhoe to remove layer upon layer to reveal your gift and purpose."

Rachel finds Grandma Ashlar's statement clever but also uncomfortable. Staring into the shimmering white-caps lapping onto the shore, she says, "Grandma, that's so beautiful, but I'm not special." Her grandmother sighs and reaches for Rachel's hand.

Her family prepares a special celebration for Rachel. There is an earthen oven on the property to smoke a whole pig. Stones are heated before the pig is placed into the oven, and the hot stones and rock salt are also added inside the abdominal and thoracic cavities of the pig. Surrounding the pig are sweet potatoes, taro root, unripe bananas, and *laulaus* (chicken and fish wrapped in ti leaf). Her brother, father, and a few calabash cousins (nonblood cousins) tend the fire. Her mother and more calabash cousins are in the main kitchen dicing up tomatoes and onions for the *lomi* salmon, while her Auntie Pauline and her crew are in another kitchen simmering the chicken, soaking the rice noodles, and cutting up the scallions for the chicken long-rice dish. Her sister, Leilani, is making the *haupia* (coconut) cake and pudding.

In between scheduled appointments, Rachel has been quiet in nature. As she walks toward the kitchen, she hears, "Keiki, come here." A silver-haired older woman calls to her.

"Tutu!" Rachel goes running toward the house.

Grandmother Alana hugs her and says, "Granddaughter, it's time," Rachel knows it must be serious because Tutu Alana never calls her granddaughter. She is dying to ask what it is time for, but she knows it's better to be silent. Instead, she follows Tutu Alana into a room where Auntie Pauline is sitting on a mat on the floor.

"Please sit," says Tutu Alana. "We have called upon our beloved *aumakua* (family guides) to come to your feast today."

"The wounded words haunt you," says Tutu Alana. She takes a cup of kava made from the 'awa root and offers it first to the ancestral spirits and then to Rachel. Tutu Alana and Auntie Pauline chant.

Rachel goes within and sees herself as a young child on the "Forbidden Isle," and she is happy. While gathering flowers, she overhears, "Her skin is too light to be learning sacred stories." Rachel knows they are talking about her because she is the only fair one on the island. Rachel feels tears of shame roll down her face.

"Rachel, let it go and open your heart," says Tutu Alana.

"Our hearts' intention is what is important, not the color of skin or eyes or hair," says Auntie Pauline. More tears stream down Rachel's face and her body feels the release. Her puffy eyes open to the two joyful smiles of her grandmother and aunt.

"Aunt Suzie's not the only one who can do a healing ceremony," says Auntie Pauline.

"We give you a new name, Maluhia. It means peaceful," says Tutu Alana.

Auntie Pauline comforts Rachel by rubbing her back and sharing these words of wisdom. "Rachel, did it ever cross your mind that Pauline is not a Hawaiian name? When we are young, we want to be like everyone else. When we grow up, we want to be different. The truth is you are unique!"

"Hurt blocks," says Tutu Alana as she touches Rachel's heart, "your heart from seeing you and your destiny."

After feasting, Rachel's brother, Kahu, picks up a gourd, taps rhythmically, and chants. Rachel's sister, Leilani, her mother, Malia, Tutu Alana, and her Auntie Pauline begin to hula. They motion for Rachel to join in. Soon strums of ukuleles and guitars join in. Rachel looks up into the starry night, feels the wind against her skin. As the moonlight skips across the water and across the faces of the people she loves, Rachel is thankful for all the help she received in coming home to herself.

Rachel returns to Tempe to gather her belongings and to say her goodbyes. She calls Angelica Mee, but Angelica is away. Packing, Rachel finds Beauregard Stickler's business card and informs him she won't be talking story with him because she is moving back to Hawaii. He offers to drive her to the Port of Los Angeles to drop off her belongings and then take her to the airport. She accepts his offer.

Rachel drives out to Aunt Suzie's and gives Aunt Suzie a traditional Hawaiian welcome. Rachel places a lei of black polished kukui nuts over Aunt Suzie's neck and then she kisses each side of Aunt Suzie's face. "This is a *kukui* nut lei and becomes more beautiful over time. With prayers, Mana, spiritual energy, goes into the kukui lei and can be used for protection. The *kukui* nut oil was used to make light in the past. I chose this for you because you are a healer and because you lit the way for me to heal my wounded heart.

"The ancestors are pleased. And my family too. I'm going home for good, and I have a Hawaiian story for you."

"We'll go to the back and enjoy the Red Mountain one last time together while you tell me the story."

They settle in. Rachel begins the story. "There is a humble farmer with supernatural energy, which Hawaiians term *kupua*. Each successful harvest, he remembers to honor Kane, the god of creation, and Lono, the god of growing things. The farmer cares for his wife, his two daughters, and his neighbors. For his reverence, the gods grant him the ability to change into a plant form upon his death. As death approaches, he ponders how he might best serve. Seeing that the people had plenty to eat, he chooses to become a special kind of tree, a mulberry tree, which would clothe the people. Before he dies, he tells his daughter to look for him and to remember two things: water and beating. The daughters follow their father's instruction and figure out how to make cloth, which Hawaiian's call *tapa*, by beating wood bark soaked in water."

Aunt Suzie smiles and says, "*Kupua* energy—the supernatural forces of the ancient ones. This is soulful work. Does this mean you will be learning sacred stories?"

Rachel nods yes and smiles. "I guess you're right. I am one tough cookie." They both laugh.

Rachel's possessions are loaded onto her pickup truck and Bo's hitches her truck to the back of his truck. They head out for Los Angeles. On the drive out, Rachel learns Bo is enamored with Polynesian culture. It comes from living in New Zealand. She tells him that Maori and Hawaiian are sister languages. Bo tells her he might come to Hawaii for an engineering project. He asks if there might be an opportunity to hear her and any of her family's stories.

Rachel reciprocates his generosity, but doesn't make any promises. "Let me know when you come to Hawaii, and my family and I will show you the meaning of aloha."

7

Bo A Strickler: What's in a Name?

Bo Strickler opens the door to his mother's home in Pacific Grove, California, where he has been living since his divorce and the death of his father. Bo has worked tirelessly, managing project after project. Carlene, his older sister, took over the engineering company, and Conrad, his younger brother, is completing his engineering degree.

Most evenings, Bo gets home late. He enjoys sitting and looking out at the stars and the moon over the Pacific Ocean. But this particular day he comes home early at the request of his mother, Veronica. "Conrad and Carlene will be here soon, so Bo, if you want to clean up, you best hurry." Bo's tall frame of six feet two inches towers over his mother, who is five feet three inches. She touches the hair above his lip. "Your Tom Selleck mustache doesn't go with your mullet. You might want to shave it off."

He hangs a pair of clean jeans and a Ralph Lauren lavender polo shirt on the back of the bathroom door. He removes his leather work boots, strips off his acid-washed jeans and powder blue t-shirt, and steps into the shower. He towels off and stands in front of the mirror. Should he or shouldn't he shave his mustache? He can't decide. He follows his mother's suggestion and the mustache is gone.

Bo returns to the family room amidst a conversation about the family business. They rarely talk about anything else these days. "Bo, I see you are wrapping up the Thompson project," says Carlene.

"Holding to Samuel Strickler's motto, 'On time and within budget.'"

"Your father built a successful engineering company on that simple formula," replies Veronica. "Thank goodness he knew how to anticipate."

"Between Dad's life insurance policy and Bo's hard work, we will keep Dad's dream alive," says Carlene.

"We've all worked hard," says Bo.

"But Dad's dream is my dream, too," says Conrad.

"And mine," adds Carlene.

His siblings look at him and his mother asks, "Is it your dream, Bo?"

"I guess."

"Jolene Diamond certainly thought so," spews out Carlene.

Bo turns his green eyes to the wooden floor. "Yeah, if only I had known our marriage was a business contract, then I might not have personalized her leaving me for someone else."

"In the days of Jane Austen, men selected their mates based on wealth and status," says Veronica.

"I think you can do better than Jolene," says Conrad. "Maybe find someone better suited to you and your dream . . . once you discover what it is."

Veronica lights up and says, "Yes, Bo, you need to go and find your dream. That's what we'll do. We'll send you on a sabbatical just like a college professor on a special assignment to find your dream!"

With skepticism, Bo asks, "Buutttt . . . what will I do?"

"Bo, you are logical as well as creative. It's time to explore your artistic side," says his mother.

Carlene comes to Bo's aid. "Begin your sabbatical with a visit to Delaware. There is an upcoming bid for a proposal on a bridge that you could check out."

Veronica frowns at Carlene but backs off when she sees Bo's face light up. "I know how much you love stories. Why don't you visit my cousins Patty Mae and Arlin Davis in Tennessee and learn some family history and stories?"

"Mom, this isn't another push like the creative writing class in college?" asks Bo.

"But you loved that class! If it weren't for that class you wouldn't have met Daniel, your best friend."

"Mom, he likes to be called Dec." Bo tries to warm to the sabbatical idea. After all, his mother is rarely wrong where he is concerned.

Dec invites Bo to a men's retreat in the Santa Cruz Mountains. Bo suspects his mother has a hand in it. "I have several English teachers, a playwright, a musical director, a lawyer, a Vietnam-veteran-turned-cowboy-poet who actually works on a cattle ranch, and a pharmacist-turned-detective. I think an engineer with a creative writing background would be the perfect addition."

Bo wavers. "Is this like a touchy-feely thing?"

"Bo, my buddy, it is all about self-discovery, self-exploration, and self-direction . . . we're preparing for the 1990s . . . a brave new world for men using both their intellects and their hearts!"

With uncertainty, Bo blurts out, "You think I'm up for that?"

"Are you kidding me? You were born for it."

Bo gives in to Dec's buoyant energy. "You must have graduated at the top of your class from the Norman Vincent Peale School of positive thinking."

"I come by good mojo naturally. So, get on board, little buddy," says Dec, even though he is four inches shorter than Bo. "Bring a journal with plenty of blank pages, so you can record your insights and perhaps release your playful inner child."

"Inner child?!" shouts Bo.

Dec explains the inner child is the creative, playful part of the self. Dec becomes excited as he shares that William Wordsworth and William Shakespeare believed in children's imagination.

"I think my inner child is lost."

"That's why you, my engineer/artist, need to come to the retreat! We'll drum and find our primal selves. We'll share personal stories and find our inner purpose and vitality."

"Dec, that's a lot to accomplish in a weekend."

Dec sighs. "Bo, you got to start somewhere. I can feel you, buddy. You are floundering at the bottom of the sea."

Bo doesn't see himself that way, but those closest to him do. He agrees to attend the retreat.

When the drum stops, Bo hasn't found his primal self. What he sees are his fellow participants sitting in silence, waiting for the first story to enter the circle. As people share their stories, Bo is stumped trying to decide what story he should share, when his name story comes to mind. Bo elaborates how his older sister by two years got a full name, Carlene Elizabeth Strickler, and his younger brother by two years got the complete name Conrad Strickler, with no middle initial. He is the middle child in the family, with a capital A with no period behind it. Bo poses the question to the group whether they think his incomplete name is the cause for a lack of clear dreams or the loss of his inner child?

"Daniel Edward Curtis—DEC—is a full name. Three first names or three last names can be confusing. The key is not to be distracted, but to stay focused and be aware. Children come into the world with total awareness. Unfortunately, the current educational system does not build on a child's natural abilities. William Wordsworth and William Shakespeare believed in children's imagination, and so do I. I have formed an educational consulting business with the specific goal of helping children use their innate gift of imagination to reach their full potential."

"Oh, those societal demons," says the cowboy poet. "Pop the head open, pour the knowledge in, not important for everyone to go within and claim the win." He grabs his journal and pen and writes. "Grab it while it's here."

"Societal constraints would be a good theater piece," says the playwright. "You know Dec is always saying ask for what you need. I tested the theory and it works."

"I love teaching and I need help with teaching the five-paragraph essay for writing. It's all form and no substance. Talk about dead looks in the students' eyes. Dec, if you need help, let me know," says one of the English teachers.

The other English teacher asks, "Did anyone see the PBS series on *Joseph Campbell and the Power of Myth* with Bill Moyers? It was electrifying. What a storyteller that man is!"

"Trial lawyers have influenced jurors by telling well-crafted, heartfelt stories," says the lawyer.

"The stories I've heard have landed people in prison," says the detective and the other men laugh.

Bo listens to the natural rhythm of the men's sharing. They feel honest. His name story seems superficial, but he knows it's all he has at the moment. Then a line comes to Bo. He is caught in the reeds while the others are riding in the open waters. He picks up his journal and jots down the line. It's a start.

Dec addresses the group. "I want to thank everyone for coming because these retreats help me to focus and fuel up."

Focus and fuel up sounds like a breakfast cereal slogan. Bo chuckles to himself. The group grows silent and reflective. Bo feels a pressure building in him. He stammers. "Ahhhhhhh, I'm just beginning this life dream business, and I don't have a clue where to begin."

The guys give Bo plenty of space to sit with his feelings and situation. The group's silence makes Bo uneasy. He feels compelled to fill it. He remembers what the playwright had just shared. "Perhaps, this would be a good time to ask you all for help."

"Once I was on a stakeout. I was reading an article about shamrocks when a truck with a big shamrock came by. Something inside of me said follow that truck, which I did, and it led me to where the deal was going down. I never told my boss, but hey, it's how it works," says the detective.

"My therapist tells me to look for patterns," says the playwright.

"Spend time in nature," says the cowboy poet. "Have you noticed how even this retreat is in nature and how wonderful it feels?"

"Build a community of people who support you," recommends one of the English teachers.

Dec smiles and says, "Keep your mind and heart open, and unrelated events will appear to reveal your dream. It's why I give these retreats."

Bo nods and thinks to himself, *I wonder how many other reasons Dec has for having these retreats.* He smiles and thanks everyone for their help, even though it wasn't all that helpful.

Bo returns from the retreat with a surprise from his mother. With a happy grin, she holds up VHS tapes of *Joseph Campbell and the Power of Myth* with Bill Moyers. "We'll see one tape a night. I think this will be a good way to send you off on your sabbatical." Bo can't believe it! This is the synchronicity that Dec spoke about, but he knows in science synchronicity is applied differently.

Bo is astonished at how compelling and magical the stories told by Joseph Campbell are. Campbell's folktales remind Bo of one of his mother's art pieces.

"Hey, mom, do you remember your watercolor of the fairy fort with the bridge melting into the sky? That painting was like stepping right into a fairytale or folktale."

Veronica studied art in college. When she married Samuel and had children, she turned her attention to watercolor because it was the easiest medium to tote. Veronica leaves the room and returns with a twelve-by-eight-inch watercolor painting of the fairy fort and bridge and hands it to her son. "Of all my children, you are the only one that ever asked me about the bridge. You are more like me than you know. It's time to explore the creative child who wonders. Socrates once said, 'Wisdom begins in wonder.' Take this painting with you as inspiration to find joyful ways to fulfill your dream."

In late summer, the Strickler family sends Bo off. Carlene and Conrad hand a list of places for Bo to investigate for the business: Delaware, a bridge project; Texas, a treatment plant; Arizona, freeways; and Colorado, an airport. His mother gives him the contact information for her cousins in Tennessee. He promises to stay in touch with phone calls.

In Lewes, Delaware, Bo parks his black Dodge Ram pickup truck at a place where he is renting a room in a house within walking distance from the center of town. He explores the town. His stomach growls, so he enters an eatery and spots two old-timers and a baby. They seem jovial, so he chooses a table nearby them. Looking over the menu, he hears, "I know you'll have to kill me if you tell me." Bo is taken aback and looks up. "Joe, don't be playing with your grandson saying those kinds of words," replies a bald-headed man with a medium frame and muscular build and light-brown eyes.

"Monty, you say that to me all the time," replies the silver-haired man with the peppered mustache and coal-black eyes who is gently rubbing the baby's head.

"It's a professional hazard for me. Besides, you're an adult." The bald-headed man leans toward the baby and sticks his finger out to entertain the infant.

Bo stares at the bald-headed man whom the other guy called Monty. "I don't mean to eavesdrop, but are you a spy?"

The silver-haired man answers. "This here is Monty and he might have to kill you if he answers that question."

Monty speaks for himself. "What would you do if I said I was a hit man?"

The two men burst out laughing. "Hey, Monty, we've reeled in a live one. By the way, I'm Joe. This is Monty, and this is my grandson Brady. We charge a fee for entertaining people."

"I'll pay if you answer my question," says Bo.

"Monty is a retired spy," replies Joe.

"But the code of secrecy is for life," replies Monty.

"For real," says Bo.

Monty asks, "By the way, who are you?"

"I'm Beauregard Strickler, but call me Bo."

"And what brings you to town?" asks Joe as he plays with his mustache, which the baby finds fascinating.

"I'm doing research on a proposed bridge," answers Bo.

"So, it's strictly business then?" asks Monty.

"No, I get to play too," replies Bo.

"Now we're getting somewhere. While you're here you need to see the Overfalls Lightship," says Monty. "Did you know that of the 179 lightships that were built from 1820 to 1952, only seventeen remain and one is located in Lewes, Delaware? But if you're interested in lighthouses, you can see two from the ocean side of Cape Henlopen."

"Monty is a volunteer and belongs to the Overfalls Lightship Society," says Joe. "So, he knows what he is talking about."

"Being locals, where might I find out about the history of the area?" asks Bo.

Joe gives Bo directions to the local place where archival information is housed.

Bo hopes he will see them again. After his meal, he heads for the local library. He goes to the reference librarian and finds information on the archive center and history of the area. The next day, he goes to the archive center and talks to the archeologist. The information and stories he hears from the archeologist help Bo to visualize the look of the bridge. He knows this is a project they can do.

Bo walks by the eatery where he met Joe, Monty, and Brady, in hopes of seeing them again, but they're nowhere in sight. Since this is a beautiful day, he decides to drive out to Cape Henlopen State Park to visit the Atlantic Ocean and two lighthouses: one sits on the Delaware Bay and another lighthouse sits on the Atlantic Ocean.

Walking back to his truck, Bo hears, "If I tell you, I'll have to kill you." Bo turns his head in the direction of the voice. He can't believe his eyes. *It's them!*

They spot him and motion him over. Bo arrives to see Monty is doing something funny with his right arm.

"Bo, do you have children around you?" asks Joe.

"No," replies Bo.

"Babies are a hoot," replies Joe.

"We've all done it, but I don't remember," says Monty.

"Bo," says Joe. "Watch my Brady here and tell me what you see."

Bo watches Brady moving his tiny fingers and toes. "Do you think Brady knows those appendages belong to him?"

"Pretty amazing, isn't it? The level of trust babies have," replies Monty and then he leans toward Bo and says, "Don't you wonder when it disappears?"

"I've been observing Brady from day one. Huge learning curve! He has a body that's difficult to maneuver. He can't lift his head; he can't roll over. He's months away from crawling and a good year from walking," says Joe with a breeze moving through his silvery hair. "But my

Brady here made a wise choice in selecting his parents and grandparents."

"Oh Joe, there you go again, gettin' philosophical, bordering on mystical. Where does it come from? You're a retired accountant, after all," says Monty as he shifts his baseball cap.

"Can't help it, it's in my blood," replies Joe.

"Bo, don't pay any attention to us. We're just two old farts," says Monty.

But Bo admits that he hoped to see them again, so he could thank them for all their help. The archeologist at the archival place told some great stories, and his family will submit a bid on the bridge.

"If stories are what you looking for, young man, we have a pile of them," says Joe. "There are even some that Monty can tell without killing you."

Bo indicates he wants to hear more stories, so Monty hands Bo a fishing pole. "You have to help catch dinner while we share a few tales about growing up in Modesto, California. Joe and I met in first grade."

Bo bids Joe and Monty good-bye before heading for Tennessee. Bo tells them he hopes they will share their stories with their families. Joe replies he plans to video record some stories for Brady, but for his own kids he's sure they're tired of his stories. Monty looks directly at Bo. "You need to come up with more of your own stories." Bo blushes and admits it's time to go beyond his name story. Monty and Joe nod in agreement and wish Bo safe journeys.

Arlin and Patty Mae Davis whisk Bo and one of their oldest storytellers in the community to Jonesborough,

Tennessee. The legendary teller is being featured at the National Storytelling Festival. Bo sits saturated in stories from 10 A.M. to midnight for three days. He discovers the magic of listening to folktales, myths, and personal stories.

Patty Mae and Arlin Davis are twins and are older than his mother by ten years. They're slim with beautiful silvery gray hair. Arlin is five feet eleven inches in height while Patty Mae is five feet eight inches in height. Arlin wears jeans and a plaid Western shirt, and Patty Mae, a denim jumper with a red t-shirt.

Sitting on the porch, Patty Mae says, "I think your mama is like Grandma June. They love to express themselves. At sixteen, Grandma June nabbed your Grandpa Jimmy and they headed west until they ran out of real estate."

Bo mentions that his mother wants him to hear some family history. Patty Mae proceeds to share how their ancestors came from England to make their fortunes and with them came folktales of a good-natured boy name Jack, like in the beanstalk. While Patty Mae shares a few Jack tales, Bo marvels at the travels of Jack from England and Ireland to the hills of Tennessee.

Arlin decides he has something to add. "Your momma shouldn't leave it up to us to let you know where you come from or how many people travel with you. Bo, tell your momma to come out here herself."

Bo's eyes light up. "Wait a minute. I have a bit of mother with me." Bo retrieves the painting from his truck and explains that his mother painted this picture in Ireland. This scene is of a fairy fort, a place where fairies supposedly pass through. His explains his mother wanted to connect heaven and earth, so that is why the bridge is there.

Patty Mae studies the painting. "We have wooded places like that! I guess I don't have to go to Ireland now."

"I feel sprite energy just like in a fairytale," declares Arlin. "No doubt about it. Grandma June travels with your momma. Does your momma travel with you?"

Bo says that his mother would say she does and he sighs. Then it dawns on him and an idea pops into his head. "You don't suppose that our story might be our legacy to life?"

"My, my, doesn't Bo have a way with words?" cries Patty Mae.

Then Arlin inquires, "And what kind of legacy are you leaving, Bo?"

Bo's face gives a look of frustration. "I wish I knew. I guess it would help if I had a dream."

"So, what has your life been saying up to now?" asks Patty Mae.

Bo squirms. "I don't know. I feel sort of left behind."

Patty Mae rocks in her chair and hollers, "You know what don't kill you will make you stronger, my granny used to say." Arlin shares that the best stories have come to him after he stood toe to toe with and stared down his doubts and obstacles.

Bo rolls his eyes upward and shares that he considers himself more like Jack of the Jack tales. Jack just bumbles into adventures and comes out better than all right. A thought from the retreat pops into Bo's mind and he shares it. "And I learned recently that help comes to those who ask for it."

"Since you're in the business of asking, how about asking to know how extraordinary your story is?" suggests Patty Mae.

Bo turns pink and laughs. "I should have thought of that myself."

"Not at all," answers Patty Mae.

"When it's sitting on your face, everyone but you can see it. That's what family is for," laughs Arlin.

Bo bids goodbye to Arlin and Patty Mae and heads for Texas to check out the treatment plant proposal and discovers that Dec is headed there, too. They agree to meet up in Dallas. As soon as Dec enters the truck, he explains he is desperate to get to Tempe, Arizona, to the Marcum G. Garver Foundation and Research Center to check out a grant proposal. The deadline is short. He asks if they could go there right away. If Bo can't, Dec will fly to Phoenix and rent a car. Bo wants to help his friend out. "Look, I have freeway projects in Phoenix to check out." So, the two guys head off for Tempe, Arizona.

On the road, Bo shares his recent discovery of how each person's story is a legacy to life. He arrived at this conclusion after listening to hours of stories from people he met in Delaware, his weekend at the National Storytelling Festival, and his time with his mother's cousins.

Dec listens and makes a comment. "You've always had a gift for language, and I don't mean technical writing, either. I've wondered why you never developed it. Perhaps story is the doorway."

"I am enamored with stories," declares Bo. "I get transported away."

"You know, Bo, stories have found their way into my world, too. I don't lecture; I tell stories. In my workshop with teachers and principals, I have them tell stories about their passion for education. It's remarkable. They become a community, and roles and positions drop away. It's like touching the real us for a moment."

"Now if only I can figure out what I am supposed to do with story. Don't make me ask the universe or make me discover it on my own," pleads Bo and knows he shouldn't have said it. "Sorry, that just slipped out."

Dec can feel that his friend is in a tailspin. He wants to be helpful and suggests that Bo expand his story repertoire.

"Et tu, Brutus. So I guess you think stories are tied to my dream," answers Bo.

Dec realizes he isn't the first to make this recommendation. He throws his hands in the air. "Hello. Everywhere you go, there's story. If it were me, I would see story as a sign and make story a big part of my life. But I am not you!"

Bo hits his head and cries out, "I should have had a V-8!"

"Little buddy, your humor is your saving grace, but also your distraction. Have you ever considered going for help?" asks Dec.

"You mean like a therapist?"

"Yeah, a good therapist can point out patterns and themes in your life, provide strategies, and help discover dreams."

"That so . . . so you really think I should be doing that?" says Bo.

"Stop! Pure and simple, it's your job to decide what is right for you!" Dec picks up a book to cut off the conversation.

Bo knows his friend is upset because Dec's book is upside down. Bo feels bad. He doesn't mean to aggravate Dec. He can't help it if Dec is so far ahead of him. Bo loves being around Dec's positive energy. Bo remembers a quote that said to leave the world a better place than we found it. He was sure his friend Dec would, but could he?

As they come up the I-10 near Casa Grande, Dec gets excited. "We're close to Tempe and the Marcum G. Garver Foundation and Research Center. Did I tell you that this foundation is dedicated to the mind, body, and spirit of children? I couldn't believe it when I heard they are researching new education models that are child centered, using the whole brain. You know, telling stories is a whole-brain activity," says Dec with dreamy eyes.

Bo doesn't want to say anything to dampen his friend's enthusiasm. "Sounds good and right up your alley."

Dec rolls his eyes and smirks. "Wouldn't it be a hoot if it was yours too?"

"What made you say that?" Bo holds his breath and watches Dec's reaction.

"It just popped into my head and out of my mouth. Sometimes, I'm just an instrument, and I give messages to others." Dec eyes Bo. "Don't ask. We're not going there!"

They roll into Tempe and head to the Marcum G. Garver Foundation and Research Center. As Bo parks his truck, Dec asks Bo if he wants to go in with him. Bo feels it is safer for him to stretch his legs and go for a short walk. Bo finds a greenbelt path. He can't believe this lovely spot in the desert. He sees individual patio homes. He finds a community clubhouse and swimming pool. He sees a sign pointing to the office. So he decides to investigate. As he opens the door, there is middle-aged man sitting there who asks, "Can I help you?"

"You wouldn't have any furnished places that I could rent for a while?" asks Bo.

"You're in luck. A casita just came open. It's cheaper if you take out a longer lease than week to week. Do you want to see the place?"

As they walk to the place, Bo asks, "What do you know about the proposed freeways for this area?"

"They are long overdue! In 1979, we had a 200-year and 500-year rain flood that closed the I-10, our one and only freeway. With only two bridges to get across the Salt River, it was a mess!" says the man with gusto and opens the door to the patio home.

Bo looks around and without hesitation says, "I'll take it! Can I move in today?"

On the way back to the office, Bo asks, "How did the City of Tempe gets its name?"

"I heard some guy passing through thought this place reminded him of the Vale of Tempe in Greece! Go figure," says the man. Bo decides to sign a lease for six months.

Bo holds up a key to Dec, who is leaning against the car going through the grant packet. "I found lodging for us tonight. I rented a fully furnished place for six months. Let's unload our gear." The casita is on Palo Verde Street. Bo gives a tour of the two tiny bedrooms, one bathroom, a small kitchen, and a combined living-family room. A small, oval, walnut dining table sits in the space between the kitchen and living-family room. The sofa is burnt orange a with brown La-Z-Boy chair.

Dec gives his nod of approval. "Your mother's painting would go well over the dining room table where you might be writing. I can't believe how fast you got this place, and it is so close to the Marcum G. Garver Foundation and Research Center."

Bo tells his friend, "Mi casa, su casa."

"Thanks buddy. You know I've got your back, too," says Dec, and Bo nods yes.

Tempe is spread out in comparison to Lewes. Bo visits the Arizona Department of Transportation and gets information on the proposed freeway projects. He researches the history, the politics, and any cultural sites that the proposed freeways might impact.

He gets acquainted with the area by joining a writing group and attending a storytelling festival in the Bradshaw Mountains. The storytelling circle feels familiar, which relaxes Bo and emboldens him to go first. He's surprised how easy it is for him to listen, and he's fascinated by Rachel Taylor, her cultural heritages, and her profession. He approaches her, only to learn she is busy with a humongous project, but he manages to show his appreciation by sharing how important archeological reports have been to his work. His efforts are rewarded as she accepts his business card.

Sitting at the community pool, Bo hears a word he hasn't heard since he was a kid in Australia, which leads to meeting Dr. Eviann Adams. He is enthralled by her when he learns she is interning at the Marcum G. Garver Foundation and Research Center. Bo can't help but wonder what makes this place so special. He hears Dec's voice saying, "Synchronicity. Pay attention!"

His usual position is listening, but not today. He's the one talking. Bo finds Eviann to be very adept in reversing the roles. At least he manages to convince her to meet him at the Community Club Café, so he can reclaim his natural listening position and hear her stories.

Bo is tickled to hear how synchronistic events have brought Eviann to Arizona. He can't wait to tell Dec. When she shares how there is magic in sharing one's story as well as listening to a story, he wonders if he felt story magic when he told his stories to her. He decides that he did feel that magic, and that Eviann reminds him of someone.

Bo finds Eviann comfortable, which brings out his chatty side. He is in disbelief when he discloses all his failed relationships on their first walk around the complex. He tries to diffuse the intensity with humor, but ends up digging a bigger hole by blaming her. Thank goodness she lightens the mood by mentioning Pablo Mora and his math camp. Bo recognizes immediately that Dec will be over the moon about this math camp. He can't believe how wonderful Eviann is for presenting this opportunity.

Pablo Mora suggests meeting in the Superstition Mountains parking lot and hiking the First Water trail. Bo arrives early and waits. Slowly, the parking lot fills up. Bo sees a Hispanic man emerging from a Toyota pickup truck wearing a huge sombrero with a number five on the front of the hat. Bo walks toward the vehicle. "Pablo Mora?"

Pablo shakes Bo's hand and explains that he wore his High 5 math hat so that Bo could easily identify him. Bo laughs. "It worked, and it's quite an art piece, too." Pablo puts his hat back in the truck, and the two men head toward the trailhead. The path to the First Water Trail is dusty, gravelly, and gradually inclines. Making their ascent, Bo asks, "How did you come up with the idea for an outdoor math program?"

"Are you familiar with the African folktale of Anansi, the spider? Anansi loves stories, but Nyami, the sky god, keeps all the stories in a box under the throne. Anansi makes a request for some stories, but Nyami isn't interested in giving any away. Not wanting to deny Anansi outright, he gives Anansi four impossible tasks to accomplish. Anansi seeks the advice of his smart wife, Aso, to solve each task, but Anansi interrupts her before she finishes because he catches the drift and knows what to do. When Anansi receives the box of stories, he shares the stories with the world. Well, I used to come home and talk to my very smart wife, Angelica, about the lack of enthusiasm that children had for math. I was outraged at how misunderstood my beloved math was. Angelica challenged me to do something about it. Voila, the High 5 outdoor math camp was created."

"So, what exactly happens at the math camp?" asks Bo.

"Children learn the practicality of math—for instance, the importance of fractions in cooking. One group in the kitchen made chili so hot that it brought tears to everyone's eyes. The recipe called for one-eighth of a teaspoon of cayenne pepper, but the team used an eighth of a cup instead. Well, that experience won't be forgotten!" laughs Pablo. "Another example is dividing pizza, pie, and other favorite foods into equal pieces."

As they arrive at the top of the rise, Pablo says, "Turn around, Bo, and look at the view." Bo does and sees converging canyons and mountain peaks reaching into the deep blue skies. "If you like that view, you must hike the West Fork Trail in Oak Creek Canyon in Sedona." Pablo motions Bo to sit. "Want to hear the *One Grain of Rice* folktale?" Bo nods yes and Pablo launches into the story. "In ancient India, a raja decrees the farmers in his province must give him all their rice so he can store it and distribute it during times of famine. But when famine comes, the raja doesn't help the farmers, because he is afraid there won't be enough food for him. One day, he decides to have a feast befitting his rank and position. As baskets of grain that are being carried by elephants are brought to the palace, the grains of rice fall out, and a young village girl sees the falling rice and captures it in her dress.

"A guard sees this and accuses the girl of stealing, but she denies it. She is brought before the raja and gives the grains of rice to him. Impressed by her honesty, he offers her a reward of anything she wishes, but she says she hasn't done anything to be rewarded and then says she might take just one grain of rice. The raja insists she must take more, so the girl adds she would take one grain today and, if the raja would like, she would have two grains tomorrow and four grains on the following day. So, each day would double her grains of rice. The raja thought this to be a modest reward. So at this point I asked the campers, is the reward modest?"

Bo laughs. "Aaah, the concept of doubling . . . the village girl ends up with all the grains of rice."

"Yes," replies Pablo. "The students are surprised that, by day sixteen, the girl received 32,768 grains of rice and by day thirty, the girl received 536,870,912 grains of rice."

Bo likes what he hears. "Any chance I could see your program in action? I'm a civil engineer and good in math and I love stories. If you need any help, I would volunteer my time."

"Well, I'm not in the habit of turning down free help," says Pablo.

"My best friend is an educational consultant, and I know he would love to see what you're doing. I think he would be a good ally and could help promote your program."

"Absolutely. The more the merrier," says Pablo. "It's more fun living a dream when you have people who value it, too. Keeping a child's interest in learning alive is important. Too many children have been traumatized by math. It's time to change that. I'm glad to have your help." Bo is moved by Pablo's passion and sees the importance of having a dream.

As they continue their hike, Pablo points out the tall saguaro cactus that grows only in the Sonoran Desert from central Arizona down to the coast of northern Mexico. He explains that the white flowers that bloom in May turn into a beautiful magenta fruit that native people and birds love to eat. Pablo points to a spiny stick plant. "That ocotillo plant comes to life after a rain. Tiny green leaves pop out in the spring, and vibrant red-orange blossoms hang on the top of each spine. The native people used to use ocotillo as a fence. No one is going to want to scale an ocotillo fence unless they are into pain," laughs Pablo. "So, Bo, what do think of the Arizona desert?"

Bo answers that the desert possesses a strange and weird beauty. Pablo agrees and tells Bo that the desert in particular and nature in general renew his spirit and give him energy to pursue his dream, and that is why his math camp takes place in an outdoor environment.

"When time isn't a factor, Angelica and I come up here and we just sit. She likes to bring her journal and sometimes her sketchpad, always checking for new plants. She gets that from her father, who is an expert on plants with healing properties. My in-laws are rare and real. They raised Angelica and her brother Rue to be that way, too."

"So, what is it like to be married to someone like that?" asks Bo.

"It allows me to be that way, too. The first moment I saw Angelica, I knew she was special. Her spirit was so clear. We were in Costa Rica—a nature lover's dream. When I heard her speaking fluent Spanish, I was a goner!"

Bo asks, "What do you mean by a clear spirit?"

"You know, being comfortable in your own skin," answers Pablo. Seeing Bo's glazed eyes, Pablo elaborates. "Let me speak of relationships in terms of fractions. Angelica and I are each a whole person, making our relationship two whole people. Once, I was in a relationship with a woman who shared only a half of herself. Then the best we could be is one and a half, but usually fractional people attract fractional people, so we would most likely be less. If we used multiplication, that is even more interesting. One-half times one-half equals one-quarter. Only two whole people lead to a chance of happiness in my opinion."

Out of curiosity, Bo asks Pablo how one determines if they are a whole or half or quarter of a number. Pablo answers, "That is a better question for my brother-in-law, the psychologist." Bo laughs and shakes his head in disbelief. He tells Pablo that he has heard that theme a lot lately. Pablo offers to put in a good word with his brother-in-law, if Bo wants. Bo replies he will think about it and then moves the conversation back to math camp.

Dec is elated about the High 5 outdoor math program. He calls Bo to tell him that he must thank his friend Eviann and inquires if there might be more going on between them. Bo states Eviann has a strange effect on him. Dec distances himself from the conversation by saying, "Good luck figuring it out. I should know sometime in November if I got the grant or not. I hope mi casa, su casa still holds."

Bo doesn't want to end this call on a sour note with his bewilderment about not having clear and succinct answers to Dec's inquiries or questions. "Give me the particulars, and I'll have your room ready."

Bo calls Eviann and invites her to a thank-you dinner. While preparing the meal, Bo thinks about Pablo's comment about healthy relationships, and Dec's question about his relationship with Eviann. Bo thinks Eviann must be a whole number. He is most likely a fraction. What about his ex-wife, Jolene? He doesn't know. Bo feels he must be comfortable with Eviann or he wouldn't be talking so much, but deep down Bo feels Eviann is more suited to his friend, Dec. But Bo knows that Dec would say that Eviann is in his life, not Dec's.

After dinner, he happily shares with Eviann what a wonderful connection was made between Pablo and Dec. It was like two dreams colliding. When she asks about his dream, he goes numb because he has no answer. How many times has he felt this way when Dec has asked him a question that he couldn't answer? Certainly, it is more times than he cares to count. It's always easier for him to make a wisecrack than to admit he doesn't know. He walks Eviann home and, in gratitude for all she's done, he leans in and kisses her, and it feels very nice.

On Sunday, Bo goes for a walk and finds himself at Eviann's place. He remembers the kiss and knocks on her door. When she answers the door, he acts goofy by using Australian vernacular. As they walk, she shares a metaphor from her mentor and, lo and behold, he sees a two-by-four cemented in the sidewalk. Initially, he is spooked by it, but like Dec, Eviann points out the beauty of it. Once again, he is being reminded of the importance of paying attention to synchronicity.

Bo takes Eviann to the Superstitution Mountains. Bo decides he wants to test if a whole number can hook up with a fraction. So he asks Eviann to take their relationship to the next level. Bo is so relieved that Eviann is willing to consider his request that he tells her to take all the time she needs.

She gives her answer when they next have dinner at her home. He is both intimidated and amazed at her decision-making process. Her answer makes it clear that a whole number doesn't want to be with fraction like him. He doesn't want to lose her in his life. Inspirational people like her do not come along every day, so he pleads for friendship. When she laughs, he knows their friendship is safe.

Bo goes to California for another men's retreat sponsored by Dec and also to meet with his family about the freeway projects in Arizona. At the retreat, Bo uses Pablo's math language for relationships and brings up the issue of whole numbers versus fractions in relationship. The men in the group agree that whole numbers and fractions belong in the domain of therapy. Even Bo's mother agrees with the men's assessment.

With Pablo's help, Bo gets an appointment with Dr. Rue Mee. For his first therapy session, Bo walks nervously in. He looks around and can't decide where to sit. Should he sit farthest from the therapist or closest to the therapist, perhaps in the middle?

Dr. Mee smiles and says, "Is it always this hard for you to make a decision?"

"It certainly seems so," replies Bo, releasing a nervous laugh.

"We make hundreds of decisions a day. It must be tough for you. Do I dare ask why you're here?" inquires Dr. Rue Mee with a relaxed smile.

"Well, the topic of therapy has come up multiple times recently—the last one from my own mother."

"So you want help with making decisions?" asks Dr. Mee with a slight grin.

"Actually, my family sent me on a sabbatical to find my dream, which I haven't fully discovered yet. My best friend tells me that therapists can help with that, too. Pablo believes a successful relationship relies on two whole numbers. I'm divorced. My ex-wife left me because I was too slow in achieving her dream. So, I guess I must be a fraction."

Dr. Mee summarizes for Bo. "Decision-making, your dream, and relationships are the three issues you want to address. I wouldn't be surprised if they all tied together, but I think we should begin with decision-making. There is an inventory I would like you to take. It is based on Carl Jung's work."

"I am somewhat familiar with Carl Jung. My friend, Dec, talks about paying attention to synchronicity and intuition all the time. Although in science and math, I think synchronicity and intuition are approached a bit or maybe a lot differently. However, of late, everywhere I go, Carl Jung's name pops up. I was watching the *Power of Myth* series with Bill Moyers and who does Joseph Campbell bring up: yup, Carl Jung!"

Dr. Mee laughs. "Thank you for confirming that this inventory is a good starting place."

"Can it really be that easy?" Bo asks hopefully. "I can be helped. I am curious though how my ex-wife leaving me for another man cannot be taken personally? It certainly feels personal, even though she says it isn't."

Dr. Mee looks at Bo, "What exactly did she say?"

"She married me because she thought I could deliver her dream. She thought I wanted that lifestyle, too. When she realized I didn't share that dream, she couldn't resist her boss's offer to share his high lifestyle with her."

"Why did you marry her?"

"She knew what she wanted and she asked for my help," says Bo.

"Seems rather impersonal to me."

"Doc, is that normal?"

"I think the better question is, what do you want from a relationship?"

"Why does it always come back to me?"

"Because it's your life and you should be in the center of it. Let me introduce you to the first strategy: Be Aware."

"Doc, I am aware that I have an incomplete name and, therefore, an incomplete picture of myself. My friend Dec thinks I just joke about it, but maybe there is something to it. Lately, I've been referred to as an engineer/artist. Doc, am I an anomaly?"

"Bo, I need to see a theme floating by at least five times before I can draw a conclusion. But don't worry, a picture is beginning to form. Let's wait for your inventory results. Meanwhile, start working on implementing the first strategy: Be aware."

Bo sits in awe. "You are so succinct."

"That's one of my gifts. Speaking of which, make a list of your gifts."

"I can do homework. My friend Dec always gives homework assignments before our retreat," says Bo.

"Excellent. Being . . . aware . . . is . . . important . . . for . . . calming . . . the . . . mind," says Dr. Rue Mee, demonstrating the effect that slow speech has on the nervous system. Bo is surprised how his body shifts and matches the energy of the doctor. Bo leaves with all his homework assignments.

At Bo's second appointment, he solemnly eases himself onto the middle of the couch. Dr. Mee says, "Why the long face?"

Bo exhales noisily. "I called Eviann to share that I'm seeing you. I learned that she has gotten her dream job and is leaving for Sydney, Australia." In a flat voice, Bo says, "I'm happy for her." Dr. Mee nods. In a monotone voice, Bo adds, "My friend Dec called to tell me he got a preliminary call about his grant submission. Living one's dream seems to be epidemic."

Dr. Mee gently looks at Bo. "Two people . . . an epidemic? Perhaps your two friends are only reminders of what you don't have, but are working toward. The first step is awareness. You are now aware that you consciously want to know your dream."

"You're spooky, Doc. I dreamt I was standing before three doors, uncertain what to do. Eviann rushed by me and entered the door to my left. I followed her. I shouldn't have followed her, but I did. In the end, that door wouldn't open. Soon, Dec rushed by me and entered the door to my right. I did the same thing, and I couldn't get in. Finally, I walked up to the remaining door. It opened, and I woke up."

"Waking up is good. Let's look at your inventory results." Dr. Rue Mee grins. "There are two pairs that are quite revealing. Decision-making falls under the pair of thoughts and feelings, and you are split right down the middle. This means you have no clear preference for making decisions. You think about a decision, and then you feel about it, and then think about it, and then feel about it, and so forth. You don't know which side of the fence to fall on. Dr. Jung believed it is better to have a preference. No clear preference makes decision-making difficult. I think engineer/artist is an accurate description of your dilemma. The other pair is sensing and intuition, and you have a definite preference for intuition, which could prove helpful. This brings me to the second strategy: Listen . . . for intuition."

Bo's mind is blown open. "So this is what a whack on the side of the head feels like. I could be Dr. Jung's poster child."

Dr. Mee laughs. "But Bo, you do have a strong preference for intuition. Pay attention and listen to your intuition. It doesn't matter if it is intuitive thought or intuitive feeling. Put intuition on your list of gifts, if it isn't there already."

"Doc, I need more information about intuition."

"Intuition is an inner knowing. You don't know how you know. You just do," answers Dr. Mee.

"Wow, that's so unscientific. I suppose multiple recommendations for therapy from various people would be an example of intuition at work?" asks Bo.

"Yes, but intuition communicates in many ways: a line in a book pops out at you, a thought in your head catches your attention, a whim to go someplace, someone saying something profound, you saying something profound, etc. We all can be instruments for intuition. The key is to trust this inner knowing," says Dr. Mee.

Bo pulls out a paper and writes on it. "I need to add story narrative or telling to my list of gifts. I just remembered that I heard that message a number of times: two guys in Delaware, cousins in Tennessee. Since I began this sabbatical, stories have fallen into my lap wherever I go. My buddy Dec said it is obvious to him that story is in my future."

"That's gives me an idea for a homework assignment. Have you heard the codependent joke? A codependent person dies and a sea of faces flashes before him. The normal way is to see one's own face flashing before you," says Dr. Mee.

"Does this mean I stop telling others' stories and start telling more stories about me?" asks Bo.

"Yes! Be aware and listen to where intuition has shown up in your stories," says Dr. Mee.

"Doc, you are like a magician. You get to the heart of the matter in the most unexpected way."

"Bo, thanks for the compliment, but that is what you are paying me for. You know the adage that truth will set you free, but not before your heart breaks . . . open. I can't wait to see what interesting things you discover about yourself," says Dr. Mee, escorting Bo out the door.

On his next visit, Bo walks into Dr. Mee's office with a painting and his journal and sits in the middle of the couch with purpose. "I'm sitting in the middle because I'm a middle child." Bo picks up the small painting and explains that he is the only one of his siblings who was intrigued by this painting. He sees this painting as a story painting.

Dr. Mee studies the painting. "This painting speaks to both your engineer and artist sides. In birth-order therapy, the first child belongs to the father, the second to the mother, and the third to the relationship. I think this fits you. I think you are ready for the third strategy: Trust." Dr. Mee's face breaks into a grin. "Now you have my BLT strategy."

Not missing a beat, Bo asks, "Can you elaborate on the sandwich, Doc?"

"Be aware of your heart. Listen to your heart. Trust your heart. I believe intuition lives in your heart. First be aware of what brings you peace, happiness, joy, or contentment. Second, listen or pay attention to when you are peaceful or joyful. Third, trust your heart, your inner knowing self, to guide you to what you truly want."

"Oh, wow, Doc, whack, whack, whack. But I think you cracked me open. I will apply your BLT strategy to my story narratives. Stories capture my head and my heart simultaneously."

"Yes, Bo, listening to story puts you into a light trance and takes you into the present moment where head and heart play together. Story is magic because story is whole. Bo, you are ready to fly solo. For your last session, select a symbol that reflects you."

Bo comes in with a miniature wooden model bridge and elaborates. "The bridge represents the connection between my mind and heart and between me and the larger community. My dream is to become a living bridge." Bo pauses a moment and says in a low, reflective tone, "Doc, I've put my decision-making process under a microscope and I've discovered a shortcut. If I'm captivated, intuition is present. My job is to pay attention and follow. It doesn't matter whether it is an intuitive thought or intuitive feeling. If I do this, I am using the BLT strategy without realizing it."

"Bo, that's well stated. Living your life in awareness is the dream. Stand in the center of self. It is the solid place to be on all levels of the self: physical, emotional, and spiritual."

Bo realizes and laughs. "I can't believe how hopeful I feel, even though I still don't know what my dream is. I do hope our paths will cross again."

"With life you never know, but I hope that will happen too," says Dr. Mee with a big grin and a glint in his eye.

Bo's face is filled with light and he hugs Dr. Mee good-bye.

When Bo learns that Rachel is moving back to Hawaii, he intuitively knows to offer her assistance. He hopes for stories, but is rewarded with a promise of aloha.

8

The Gathering

B o unlocks his front door and steps into his abode to find papers strewn over his dining table. He calls out to Dec, but there is no answer. He takes a peek at the reports and the studies from the Marcum G. Garver Foundation and Research Center and mutters, "BLT."

"I could do with a bacon, lettuce, and tomato sandwich," says Dec, coming through the open door.

"Actually, BLT stands for be aware, listen, and trust. It's a strategy given to me by Dr. Mee."

"Excellent! Dr. Mee's studies are pioneer stuff, but I didn't see any mention of the BLT method in her reports."

A realization comes over Bo and he laughs. "There are two Dr. Mees. The creator of the BLT strategy is Dr. Rue Mee. I think you're speaking of his sister, Dr. Angelica Mee."

The wheels turn in Dec's mind. "Bo, just now, what made you go over to the table to look at this stuff? Don't think. Use the BLT strategy and tell me."

"I was drawn to it."

"I thought so. You see I could use some help with this grant."

"Well, I was thinking about going to Hawaii for a proposed freeway project and an opportunity to visit Rachel Taylor and hear some Hawaiian stories and maybe find my way to a sacred storytelling ceremony." Bo gives a nonchalant grin.

"A sacred storytelling ceremony . . . that sounds intriguing. Bo, maybe all of this is connected. I think . . . we need to take some time to . . . " Dec couldn't finish his thought.

Bo knows his friend's mind is spinning. He can't believe it, but he knows what to do. "Let's go to Sedona for a mini-retreat." Over the evening meal, Bo shares with Dec things he has learned from his sessions with Dr. Rue Mee: how his gift of intuition and his gift of story narratives have connected his logical mind with his creative heart; how he built a model wooden bridge to symbolize the connection to his whole brain and how he hopes it will connect him to the wider community. Dec quietly sits and listens to his friend while on the inside he is doing the happy dance.

The sky is as dark as the black coffee in their individual thermoses at five in the morning. Bo starts the truck for their one-day retreat to Sedona. Dec leans back in the passenger seat and informs his companion, "Did you know that William Wordsworth was a big advocate of children's imagination?"

"You've mentioned that before," replies Bo.

"I only repeat myself when I'm tired. I'm too busy. I need an assistant to help me put together an advisory group for my project."

"I'm not an expert on children's imagination," says Bo.

"Yeah, but have you noticed you are surrounded by experts like Dr. Eviann Adams, Pablo Mora, and your own therapist, Dr. Rue Mee? And all these people know the leading expert, Dr. Angelica Mee."

Bo hasn't discerned that connection, but his friend is right. Has he already become the bridge? Bo moves into project mode and says, "So, you want to focus this day on identifying your advisory group."

"Yes, and a bit more," says Dec, as he processes aloud.

They arrive at Bell Rock. They park the truck and hustle to the first plateau just as the sun begins to rise. When they reach the second plateau, Dec tells Bo that he senses vortex energy, so they sit while the sun slowly illuminates the majestic red rocks. They remain transfixed as the light changes the hues of red, purple, pink, and beige against the sapphire sky. "Breathtaking!" utters Dec. Then he snickers and nudges Bo, "So, where are Wile E. Coyote and the Road Runner?"

"And the ACME...Company...." sings Bo. "Hungry?"

"Yes," says Dec, as he moves quickly down the Bell rock with Bo right behind him.

They have breakfast at the Cactus Café and then head off for the West Fork Trail in Oak Creek Canyon. They park off to the side of the road and make their way to the trailhead. The creek is running, but their long legs have no problems traversing the creek, and they marvel at the iridescent sunlight on the canyon walls.

Their senses take in the beauty of the waning fall foliage, and peace and balance seep easily into their souls. Dec can't believe the golden leaves pressed against the cobalt sky. He quietly declares, "Awesome!"

"I got the idea to come here from Pablo Mora," says Bo and neither of the men miss the significance of it.

At one point, they lie down on the ground so they can see the sunlight shining through thinning layers of the remaining pink, orange, and red leaves of the oak and maple trees. "To me, this is proof that God or a creative living force exists," says Dec.

Before heading home, Bo tells Dec that Oak Creek is known for its golden and red delicious apples and apple cider. But as they drive by the stands, they are shut tight, indicating they are too late. When they reach Black Canyon City, Bo tells Dec that Rock Café is known for its pies. Over a coconut cream pie, Bo agrees to help Dec by approaching Pablo Mora and Dr. Eviann Adams.

Bo makes contact with Pablo Mora. "Tell Dec I'm flattered to be on the advisory committee, but the better person would be my wife, Angelica. She is the expert in the field. When she returns from London, I'll put in a good word for you." Bo knows how effective Pablo's word can be.

Bo calculates the time difference and calls Eviann in Australia. Eviann is thrilled about Dec's project. The first question she asks, "Is Dr. Angelica Mee involved? You know she's the leading person in the field. Do you need me to put in a good word for you?"

"Pablo has offered, but it couldn't hurt if you did, too." Bo feels connectivity flowing. "Eviann, you're right, synchronicity is bloody marvelous!"

"Bo, my fiancé, Dr. Donald Nelson, is the Director of the Louise Parker Children's Research Center, and he would be good for the Advisory Committee."

"Congratulations, Eviann. Is this an either-or situation?"

"Yes, if Angelica says yes, all three of us are in," laughs Eviann.

"Very cute," says Bo. When he hangs up, he realizes that both Eviann and Dec refused to let him off the hook. They wanted him to travel his own path and find his own dream. His refusal to do so drove them mad. Thank God for Dr. Rue Mee.

Bo has been dying to call Rachel. He looks at his watch, figures out the time difference, and calls. "Howsit?" asks Bo and he hears Rachel telling him that he's being put on speakerphone since Grandma Ashlar and Auntie Pauline are present.

"Bo, this is Auntie Pauline. We hear you want to talk story. So, you talk story first."

"This is Grandma Ashlar. Yes, tell us something about you."

Bo lets intuition lead and shares the first thing that pops into his head. "I am helping my friend, Dec, put together an advisory committee for his grant to integrate children's natural abilities in education. The first person I asked recommended his wife, Dr. Angelica Mee. The second person I asked recommended Dr. Angelica Mee. I have never met her, but she is all around me. In fact, this grant belongs to the foundation where she works and where she is on their board of directors. I think an interesting story is unfolding."

"Bo, this is Auntie Pauline. Let me add more spice to this story. If Angelica Mee agrees to be on this advisory committee, we'll host you folks. You can have a retreat here. Rachel and I will even do a sacred Hawaiian ceremony. There's enough room for twenty-five people, if some are willing to sleep on the beach under the Hawaiian stars or stay in tents with air mattresses for comfort."

"Bo, this is Rachel speaking. Oahu means the 'gathering place.'"

"You would do that just to spice up a story!"

Auntie Pauline laughs. "*Aumakua* . . . our family ancestors want us to."

"Our family spirit guides," translates Rachel.

Bo happily hangs up the phone. He likes where this story is headed. It's like Star Trek meets the Ghost-busters—a good mix of science with creative humor.

Bo gives Dec an update once he hears from Angelica Mee. "Dec, do we have funds for a retreat for the advisory committee? Rachel's family has offered their property for a retreat along with a sacred Hawaiian ceremony if Angelica Mee agrees to be on your committee, which she has. She even has a recommended list of people for the advisory committee and they are as follows: John and Pepper Mee, her parents; Dr. Rue Mee, her brother; Helena Sawolynska—"

Dec interrupts. "The Russian opera singer who defected!"

"Yeah, that's the one. Payne Ow Porter—" continues Bo.

"The best-selling author! I am just dying to find why she is recommending them!"

"I wanted to know, too. She said she selected people whose gifts have been nurtured. It's time for like-minded people to come together."

"Creating my project as a living example, that's brilliant! And a novel organizational concept!" shouts Dec.

"Dec, how large can your advisory committee be? I count ten possibilities already and that doesn't include you."

"Make that twelve; I want you on the committee. Bo, we can't let money be the deciding factor. Let's play this out and see what happens. So far, so good, wouldn't you agree? I want to go to Hawaii, and I know you do, too. So, let's align our intentions to that end."

Bo watches the advisory committee grow to fifteen names: John Mee, Pepper Mee, Rue Mee, Angelica Mee, Pablo Mora, Eviann Adams, Donald Nelson, Helena Sawolyn-ska and her friend William Edward, Payne Ow Porter and his agent Scott Green, Rachel Taylor and her Auntie Pauline, Daniel Edward Curtis (Dec), and Bo Strickler.

Bo records the magic of synchronicity, which he now refers to as visible and invisible helpers. He learns Payne Ow Porter has a book signing in Hawaii in May and the publisher will be paying his way out. Bo calls Auntie Pauline for retreat availability and it coincides with Porter's dates. America West Airline has also added a new route, a nonstop flight from Phoenix, Arizona, to Honolulu, Hawaii, and is offering a promotional price of $311 round-trip. Bo jumps on the deal, only to discover that Angelica has money from another grant that will take care of her trip and that of Eviann Adams and Donald Nelson.

Bo and Dec arrive in Hawaii several days before the gathering. Rachel greets them each with a tuberose/carnation lei and a kiss on each cheek. Riding back, Rachel teaches Bo and Dec how to pronounce Hawaiian words. "See that word," pointing to the highway sign.

"The Likelike Highway," says Dec.

"Yes, that one, which is pronounced leekayleekay, not likelike," says Rachel.

"So, the vowel i is e and e is a?" asks Dec.

"Yes," answers Rachel.

"I find vowel languages very melodic to the ears," says Dec.

"And I love hearing Hawaiian music," says Bo. So Rachel turns the radio on.

"Is that a love story to the morning dew?" asks Dec.

"Eddie Kamae drew the inspiration for this song from his beloved hometown of Waimea on the Big Island, which can be damp and chilly. It is not unusual for us to sing songs and hula to honor the land and the people," answers Rachel.

"Well, I'm touched by the sentiment," says Dec and turns to Bo. "I didn't know you liked Hawaiian music."

"You don't know everything about me. I am full of surprises, even to myself!" says Bo with an impish grin.

"Now, that I *do* know about you," guffaws Dec.

"We're headed toward the windward side of the island. We'll pass the Pali cliffs, and, if you look carefully, you might catch a few waterfalls," says Rachel. Bo and Dec become quiet as they look out the windows to see the deeply carved grooves in the mountains made by years of falling water.

When they arrive at the retreat site, Rachel introduces Bo and Dec to her aunt. "This is my *anake*, or Auntie Pauline." Bo and Dec see a sturdy-framed, statuesque woman wearing a colorful muumuu; she has striking silver hair, stylishly cut to frame her face. Her smooth olive complexion gives her a youthful look, and it is hard to guess her age.

Auntie Pauline places a kukui nut lei around the necks of Bo and Dec and gives them both a kiss. In a soft but firm voice, she says, "Call me Auntie Pauline. Everyone does. *Kaukau*," and she makes a motion to eat. "After we *pau* eating, we'll tour the place. Is that okay with you?"

Bo and Dec indicate they need to stretch their legs first after a long plane ride. So Rachel and Auntie Pauline take them on a tour of the property. "This family estate belongs to Hawaiian Trust, a private organization dedicated to keeping Hawaiian culture alive," says Auntie Pauline.

As they walk, a small grove of trees grabs Bo's attention. He walks around and studies them carefully. He scratches his head. "Pineapples grow on the ground, not on trees, right?"

Auntie Pauline laughs, "Those are Hala trees. Those pineapple-looking plants dry and fall off the tree, and are used to become many paintbrushes. You can paint with them, but Hawaiian artists don't use them today. They're not so good. Nowadays the leaves are dried and woven into mats, rugs, and purses," says Auntie Pauline.

"Also known as scientifically as *Pandanus odoratissimus*," adds Rachel.

Dec looks on the ground and picks up a few of the pineapple-like plants and hands them to Bo.

As the group moves a little farther from the grove, Bo and Dec get really excited when they see a thatched structure. Dec asks the obvious, "Is that a real Hawaiian hut?"

Bo points to another structure and asks, "Is that where the sacred dances and ceremony are held?"

Auntie Pauline answers Dec first. "That hale is an old Hawaiian grass hut. It was built to help the *keiki*, the young ones, feel at home when visiting their *kupuna wahine* or *kupuna kane*, who keep the traditional ways."

Rachel laughs, "If you go to Waikiki, you find many souvenirs on coffee mugs and t-shirts, but they will not say *kupuna wahine* or *kupuna kane*, it will say *tutu wahine* or *tutu kane* for grandmother and grandfather."

"I love hearing the Hawaiian language," says Dec. "It's like listening to lovely music."

"*Akamai* for a *haole*," says Auntie Pauline.

"Smart for a white guy," translates Rachel.

"Sounds better in Hawaiian than English," laughs Dec.

Bo couldn't contain his curiosity and inquires, "And the other place?"

"That is a special place for hula, our sacred dances," says Rachel.

"Let's *hele on*," says Auntie Pauline, motioning them to hurry along and follow her. "I think Bo has waited long enough." They hike a ways when they come to an area like a mini-amphitheater that faces a large, shallow cave wall. Ironwood trees surround the side that leads to the beach, and a few bamboo trees surround the other side. Auntie Pauline looks at Bo and nods her head.

Bo takes in the place. He closes his eyes for several minutes. When he opens his eyes, he says, "It is so peaceful and secluded. I feel I've been transported to another world."

"Auntie Pauline," says Dec. "Can we go over our schedule today and will you tell us when it is best to do the ceremony?"

Bo's ears snap to attention. Auntie Pauline nods in the affirmative and motions them toward the grove of ironwood trees and she says, "*Makai*."

"I know an island is surrounded by water, but in Hawaii, we give directions by going toward the ocean, *makai*, or going toward the mountains, *mauna*," explains Rachel.

When they move past the ironwood trees and onto the fine sandy beach, Dec can't contain himself. He removes his shoes and runs toward the clear blue-green waters of the warm Pacific Ocean with Bo following behind him. The two guys let salt water skim over their feet and kick water up to splash each other. When the two return, they notice how the ironwood trees provide shade. Dec pokes Bo and says, "This would be a good place for a storytelling circle."

Bo concurs and turns to Rachel. "All the objects will be placed in the middle of the circle. We'll need more special objects to augment those brought by the participants. Can you help with what we can use to place the objects on and find a few more objects for those who didn't bring one?"

"Off the top of my head, we could use beach mats. Everyone can carry one. Everyone's mat can be like a spoke of a wheel with each sitting on one end and the objects placed in the center of the wheel. And, special objects, what about what you are holding in your hand and the *kukui* lei around your neck?" suggests Rachel.

"I love it. Are there other natural Hawaiian objects?" asks Bo.

"Yes, no problem," replies Rachel.

As the four near the house, Auntie Pauline points out where the participants can sleep in the house, on the lanai, in tents, or under the stars on the beach. She shows them outdoor and indoor showers and toilets. Auntie Pauline explains a few calabash cousins have volunteered to prepare the retreat meals, but thought it might be fun for participants to assist with preparing the luau. "For sure, everyone will want to see the pig prepared in the traditional Hawaiian way. Afterward, we'll sing and dance."

Bo uses his head to point to Dec. "This one tells me I can't carry a tune. But since this is such a magical place, maybe I will sound better."

"Anything is possible," laughs Auntie Pauline.

Dec looks around and feels blessed. He wants to express his deep gratitude in Hawaiian . . . "Auntie Pauline and Rachel, thank you very much," so he says, "*Mahalo nui loa.* I hope I didn't butcher that too badly."

Auntie Pauline smiles and asks, "*Kau kau?*" This time, Bo and Dec don't need a translation. Inside the house, they spot a woman with white hair leaning over a Crock-Pot. "Grandma, this is Bo Strickler and Daniel Curtis," says Rachel. Rachel hugs her grandmother and says, "Bo and Dec, this is my Grandma Ashlar. She has prepared some *pupus,* appetizers, for us." Rachel peeks into the pot. "Oh, yum! Gram made Swedish meatballs." Then Rachel laughs. "I think Gram feels you might need a side of Nordic cosmology and of the nine different worlds to go along with the meatballs."

Grandma Ashlar places a platter of meatballs and bread on the table and with a twinkle in her eye says, "The role of Goddesses in Nordic mythology is matriarchal, not unlike the Hawaiian culture."

"Well, Gram, who doesn't love Freya, the Goddess of love, beauty, fertility, war, wealth, divination, and magic?" says Rachel.

"Freya reminds me of Hina and Pele," says Auntie Pauline.

"I'm not messing with strong feminine power. Count me in as supporter," says Dec.

"*Akamai,*" says Auntie Pauline.

"I remember that means smart," says Dec, giving Rachel a wink.

Bo gives two thumbs up to support feminine energy. There is no way he is going to jeopardize experiencing a sacred Hawaiian ceremony and disrespecting his mother for sending him on this adventure.

On the day of the retreat, all participants are slated to arrive by 10 A.M. The retreat itself has come together with so little effort; and yet, it is still hard to believe that this day has finally arrived. Rachel volunteers to pick up the Mee family and Pablo Mora in Kailua. Payne Ow Porter and Scott Green will drive a rented car out to the property. A van has been dispatched to pick up the participants arriving from Australia and England. Bo and Dec stay at the retreat center preparing for the day's activities and guests.

Bo and Dec are hyper-vigilant. Auntie Pauline's voice in the kitchen seems thunderous. The opening and closing of the back door seem deafening, and yet they miss it. They hear happy voices outside and rush out to see Auntie Pauline kissing a Chinese woman's cheeks and placing an exquisite flower lei made of orange petals around her neck.

"Boy, for an older woman, that Auntie Pauline moves fast," says Dec.

"And she has bionic hearing, too," says Bo.

"I wouldn't be surprised if she possesses extrasensory perception," says Dec.

"Like intuition on steroids," suggests Bo.

The two men laugh. Then they watch as another car pulls in. Two guys, about the same height, get out. One has black hair and a dark olive complexion. The other one has straight, brownish-yellow hair and is sporting a tan. The darker-complexioned fellow darts toward the Chinese woman. Then the van picking up the international folks arrives. The doors open and two women bolt out the door and run toward the same Chinese woman.

Bo looks down at his sheet and says to Dec, "I have never met her, but I bet you that is Dr. Angelica Mee. I recognize Pablo, her husband, and Dr. Rue Mee, her brother. The older couple must be her parents, John and Pepper. Of the two ladies, the auburn-haired one is Dr. Eviann Adams. Angelica is her mentor. The other must be the Russian opera singer, Helena Sawolynska." After identifying everyone, Bo asks, "What are we doing standing here? We should be where the action is."

Dec laughs. "It could be a challenge like salmons swimming upstream. Those people look determined to reach the prize of Dr. Angelica Mee. Right now, I feel we have the best spot to observe." Dec turns to Bo and says, "Let's ask to know what this connective energy means for the project and for us." They close their eyes and focus.

Bo looks at Dec. "Ready to swim upstream!"

Dec and Bo go over the day's schedule with the participants: settle in, have lunch, and gather at 1 P.M. for a short walk to begin their first activity, a storytelling circle. Bo, Dec, and Rachel arrange the circle with mini-beach chairs. Auntie Pauline nixed the individual *tami* mats idea, saying older people needed back support. So Rachel uses *tami* mats for inside the circle to protect the 4-feet by 4-feet piece of Hawaiian quilt where the special objects will be placed. Out of her backpack she pulls a conch shell, a coconut, a polished *kukui* nut, a Pandanus paint brush, a lava rock with embedded olivine crystals, and a ukulele, which she positions around the quilt. Bo and Dec sit across from each other, with Rachel making a triangle.

Dec surveys the group and begins, "Thank you all for coming. Thank you to Bo for letting his intuition take the lead and for his good organizational work. Thank you to Rachel's and Auntie Pauline's family spirit guides for hosting us. Let me briefly review the storytelling circle ground rules: One person speaks at a time. No interrupting or asking questions and no sharing another person's story without permission. At this time, whoever brought a special object may place it on the quilt. As you can see, Rachel has already added a few extras to get us started."

Payne Porter puts his jade turtle on the quilt; Pablo Mora brings out a six-inch wooden H with the number 5 next to it and places it on the quilt closest to where he is sitting; Donald Nelson lays a small geode with shiny crystals near him on the quilt. Helena Sawolynska rests the Charioteer and Fool tarot cards on the quilt near her. Eviann Adams removes from her pocket an oval pink quartz; Bo uncovers a small model bridge. Dec pulls out a toy of a Japanese boy sitting at his desk.

Seeing no more objects being placed, Dec continues. "Story prompts are helpful aids designed to fire up your memory and stimulate your imagination, or to coax a story forward. I offer three prompts, but, if none of the prompts work, then share any story that comes to mind. First prompt: Think of a story that illustrates your child's sense of wonder and delight at play. Second prompt: Think of a story where intuition or synchronicity appears in your life. Third prompt: Tell the story of why you came to this retreat.

"When you are ready to share your story, pick up one of the objects and hold it up so everyone knows the story space belongs to you. State your name to help us get better acquainted. When you're finished, put the object back on the quilt. We're a rather large group, so if we keep our story to no more than 10 minutes, it should work. I'll be quiet now." Dec sits still and waits while Bo looks around the group.

Rachel picks up the conch shell and holds it up. "I'm Ashlar Rachel Taylor. I met Angelica Isatis Mee while hiking South Mountain Park. She challenged me to live my initials, ART. Ta da!" Rachel raises her arms up. "Angelica is also responsible for me meeting Aunt Suzie, a Pima healer and storyteller. When Bo called and mentioned Angelica's name, I quietly told Auntie Pauline that this is the woman who saw my restlessness. You see, I am *hopa*, which means half. I am half Swedish and half Hawaiian. I didn't know that my Hawaiian ancestors chose me to tell the sacred stories. I turned my back on this request, not because I wasn't interested or didn't want to do it. I turned my back because I allowed others to shame me into believing that I didn't deserve it. Well, Auntie Pauline, and actually my entire family, wants to meet Angelica in person, so we offered the retreat site."

Rachel looks at Bo. "But that's not the only reason. My auntie is an elder and elders know how to listen to their family spirit guides, so they do have a hand in this. I think I've answered at least one prompt and maybe all three. I'm an overachiever, after all." Rachel places the conch shell back on the quilt.

Helena holds up her tarot cards. "I'm Helena Natalia Sawolynska and my English is coming along, but please be patient with me. I come to thank Angelica and Eviann for saving my Grandmama Irena's and my lives. I am an opera singer. Opera is filled with drama and deceit, and my real life has been, too. My mother had a KGB boyfriend. My father stole my mother's heart while the boyfriend was away. My parents died in mysterious car accident.

"When was I little, I loved to sing opera. I especially loved *Carmen*. My friend William here took me to hear an amazing gypsy violin player whose great-grandmother reads tarot cards. I found out I have gypsy blood." Helena shows the cards. "The two tarot cards are the Charioteer and the Fool. My grandmother and I picked the same two cards and from the same woman, but years apart. We are descendants of caretakers from the Library at Alexandria. The cards represent a new guiding principle, and I have no idea what it is.

"This story is interesting, yes? And even more interesting is that my friend William read in Manly P. Hall's book, *Secrets of the Ages*, about the history of the tarot cards and the Gypsies, and it confirms that what Sophia tells me is true. Sends chills, yes?" says Helena and then concludes, "I'm here because I wanted to see Angelica and Eviann again and thank them for helping me. Also, to know more about this new guiding principle and what I am to do about it." Then she puts the tarot cards down.

William holds the ukulele. "I'm William Edward. I owe so much to my grandfather, Sir Laurence Edward. He was a biologist, a diplomat, and, perhaps, in the secret service. There are rumors that he never outright denied. His extensive travels opened up new worlds to my father and me. My grandfather always made me feel that I belong to the world and the world is a part of me. I was able to tell him about this retreat before he passed away. His eyes lit up when he heard the names of John and Pepper Mee. He asked me to send his love to the entire Mee clan." William nods to the Mees.

William pauses and his eyes light up as he confesses, "I love music. I think synchronicity and intuition are amazing composers, and I am a willing instrument." William's cleverness with words makes him laugh as he returns the ukulele back to the quilt.

Pablo, with an impish smile, holds up his wooden H with the number 5. "I'm Pablo Mora, and this object represents my love for teaching children the joys of math and to not be afraid of it. I'm here because of intuition. Sounds intriguing, right? Well, it is. My mother was a novice getting ready to become a nun when my father spotted her and knew this was the woman for him. He convinced her to marry him instead of the Big Guy." The participants laugh.

"My mother has always told my brother and me that we were blessings from God. She taught us to listen and follow our hearts. And that's what I did when I saw Angelica. If I hadn't, I wouldn't be sitting here right now. Perhaps I came, too, because of this new guiding principle that Helena spoke of," concludes Pablo with a look of hopeful wonder. Pablo returns the wooden H with the number 5 back on the quilt.

Eviann hoists her oval pink quartz up slightly above her right shoulder. When she has the attention of the group, she lowers her hand and speaks, "I'm Eviann Adams and this pink quartz represents someone very special to me, my Great-Uncle Ambrose. I came because of Angelica Mee. She is my mentor and colleague. And, yes, Helena is correct; this new guiding principle has my heart. And of course, a retreat meeting in Hawaii is nothing to sneeze at." A light laughter travels around the circle.

"I truly look forward to the day when all children and their natural abilities can be seen and nurtured by adults, whether they are parents or educators. I would have loved to have experienced that for myself freely. Then, perhaps, my Great-Uncle Ambrose wouldn't have had to disguise himself as a pink light," says Eviann. "But thank God for my great-uncle, for intuition, and for synchronicity. They have all been great guides for me. If I gave a testimonial instead of a story, I do apologize. I'm just too excited to follow the rules." Then she places the oval pink quartz back on the quilt.

Donald lifts up the geode, and the light filtering through the ironwood trees causes the crystals to sparkle. "I'm Donald Nelson. While visiting the Marcum G. Garver Foundation and Research Center, I met some amazing children. Rosemary Dugan, who is five, composed this line that often runs through my mind. 'I'm mad, simply mad, with wonder and delight.' Another child there, Patrick Anderson, can see in three dimensions, and I can't wait to see what will happen to Patrick when he grows up because, you see, when I was his age, I could do the same, but there was no one there to cultivate my abilities. And I want to honor the natural child within me and am happy to join in on any efforts to promote this concept in the world. I don't know if I answered any of the prompts or not. If I didn't, I'm so sorry, too."

Rue reaches for the conch shell as Donald puts his object down. "I'm Rue Mee. A child explores the natural world with full attention. My parents allowed me to live in the present moment and explore the world with wonder and delight. I feel this permitted my intuition to come out and play and allowed our relationship to grow strong. Today we are best friends. My patients accuse me of having a sixth sense. So you can imagine my shock when I found out that most people live in the past or future and skip over the present. The irony is that intuition lives in the moment along with joy and cheerfulness. When I tell them that cheerfulness lives in Mees' DNA, they think I have gone over the edge. If you don't believe me, ask my father."

Rue looks toward John, who nods his head in confirmation. "Do you have any idea the pressure it is to have no excuse for living a joyful life? Perhaps I will develop the belly-laugh therapy to go along with our new guiding principle." Chuckles could be heard around the circle. Rue waits for the laughter to die down before speaking again. "And I'm here at this retreat because my sister, Angelica, told me to come. When my older sister speaks, I listen, and it seems I'm not the only one." Smiles spread across the faces of the participants.

Angelica reaches for the conch shell as Rue starts to put it down, so Rue passes it to her. "I'm Angelica Mee. I came into the world putting the needs of others before my own. I absorbed and carried their emotional burdens. This caused great hurt and undermined my sense of self. With love and patience, my parents helped me to see that putting me first means I believe in others and trust them to know how to travel their path. After all, Socrates said wisdom begins in wonder, and isn't it interesting that children come into the world with the natural ability to wonder, and in pure delight, no less. I believe the new guiding principle is returning to our natural way to learn." Angelica pauses and then concludes, "I came to this retreat because this is where I need to be and because I want to bring life to this new guiding principle."

John extends his hand toward his daughter, so she passes the conch shell to him. "I'm John Ming Mee. I've been surrounded by magical guides my entire life. It was they who showed me how to embrace great joy and humor. Their toys were the natural world. They were playful, not so serious about everything. Their love for me was unconditional. And because of them, the openness and innocence of a child's mind and heart never left me. To this day, I enjoy dragons and rainbows," and John winks at his wife.

Pepper looks at him and he gives the conch shell to her. "I'm Pepper Mee. My parents died when I was very young. I was raised by a Shaolin priest who was a friend of my parents. He prepared me to meet and live my destiny. I carry warrior energy, a warrior of truth. Truth is rarely popular, but is so important to growth. My entire family's destiny rode on the back of synchronicity and intuition. Oh, and I want to add that the Rainbow Dragon that my husband speaks of is our matchmaker. I learned that no task is too small for great mythical beings." Pepper looks around, but no one seems to want the shell, so she puts it back on the quilt.

Payne reaches for the jade tortoise and holds it high. "I'm Payne Porter, and I brought this jade tortoise because, like it, I'm slow but steady. I eventually get there. I want to thank Angelica for giving me a big push when I needed to swing high. So often in my life when I get stuck, someone comes to my aid. When I was four, I had a birthday party and I got an Atari video game system, which I happily shared with my party friends. But then they began to fight over the game; I got so upset that I went to my bedroom. Soon, I heard a knock on the door. It was Scott, with my friends. He made them apologize. Then I was surrounded by my friends and everything was all right again."

Payne tilts his head toward Angelica and says, "After meeting Angelica, I realized I had imprisoned myself by worrying about what others thought about me. The people who loved me tried to make me laugh. They knew I was too intense, too serious. The day I swung high, I let go. I couldn't believe how light I felt. By the way, I would be interested in belly-laughter therapy. As for synchronicity and intuition, they came knocking on my unconscious

door through my dreams! Boy, did they play with me."
Payne looks at Scott. "Today, at this very moment, I am
grateful that they did." Payne leans over and places his
jade turtle back on the quilt.

Scott Green tries to balance a coconut on his head,
but is unsuccessful. "I'm Scott Green. I'm Payne's best
friend and agent. My father is a lawyer and my mother is
a therapist. So when my mother observed me at Payne's
birthday party advising the boys to apologize to Payne for
fighting over his birthday present, she felt sure I would follow in her footsteps. My father saw it differently. He felt I
was a good negotiator like him and that I would become a
lawyer. I surprised them both and didn't do either."

A puckish expression comes over Scott. "The truth
of the matter is that I just know things. I can sense when
someone is holding back or is afraid or lying. Is it intuition? It could be. Do intuition and synchronicity have a
firm hold on me? Does it matter? It seems so to my friend
over here who believes I haunt his dreams, but I want you
to know it's always in a good way. I have his best interest
at heart." Laughter breaks out.

"No kidding, he is forever accusing me of having this
spooky extrasensory perception. Apparently, this ability seems weird to him, but, to me, it is very ordinary. I
believe we are here to use the gifts we are given. As to
what brought me here, I would say my buddy Payne and
a 747 airplane. I'll admit I have a tendency toward childlike qualities—not childish qualities, mind you." More
laughter comes from the group.

"As a child of wonder and delight, I think the best
way to promote this new guiding principle is through a
book. My 'woo woo' senses say there is at least one person
here who could write it," chuckles Scott. "I'm not joking

or teasing. I'm deadly serious. There's power in print." He eyes Payne before putting the coconut back.

Auntie Pauline picks up the conch shell and holds it high. "Aloha, everyone. I'm Auntie Pauline—yes, everyone calls me that, whether they are related to me or not.

"*Ohana* means family and family is important to me. Being Auntie Pauline allows me to be in many families like this one in the circle. *Aumakua* are our special spiritual healers and advisors to a family. Our Rachel stayed on the mainland because of past hurt. We ask our *aumakua* for help and they use the beautiful Angelica Mee to assist our Rachel. The handsome, but hungry for story, Bo, befriends our Rachel. You see how the magic works? Now I can thank Angelica in person." Auntie Pauline returns the conch shell.

Bo picks up the small wooden model bridge. "I'm Bo A Strickler. Wow, no one but my mother calls me handsome, and at times she has called me clueless. The truth is, I was indecisive because I lack a strong preference between thought and feeling." Bo hoists the bridge up so everyone can see it. "This bridge represents me. It's a bridge that connects my mind to my heart through intuition. Dr. Rue Mee helped me to see that living my life is living my dream. Since you are all here, you must be a part of my dream!

"I think my brain and heart might be on fire! But please don't anyone throw water on me and put it out! Our stories connect us somehow. They must." Bo stops a moment. "Lately, I hear myself saying that our story is our legacy to life. My life is a living story and every human life is a story to humanity. Perhaps I could be the poster child of what happens when gifts are not identified early on, developed, and nurtured." Finally, a few laughs could be heard.

After Bo returns his model bridge to the quilt, Dec reaches for the toy of a Japanese student sitting at a desk. Dec winds up the toy and the student writes madly over his desk. Everyone is tickled with delight. "I'm Daniel Edward Curtis. I had a lemonade stand when I was five, a newspaper route when I was ten, and a tutoring business when I was in college. I get my entrepreneurial spirit from my father, who had a lucrative insurance business. What excites me most is seeing eyes light up and minds open. I think I get that from my mom, who's a wonderful and inspiring English teacher. I wrote several creative pieces in high school, which got accepted and published in several teen magazines. So after graduating from college, I wanted to try my hand at freelance writing. But I needed to bring in more revenue to make ends meet. So I decided to substitute teach. This decision would change the course of my life."

Dec gets choked up and stops a moment. "It's not only criminal to see lifelessness in a child's eyes, but it breaks my heart as well. I wanted to know why this was happening in the American school system, so I began asking questions to the children themselves, my own private survey. I asked first graders, second graders, third graders, fourth graders, and fifth graders all the same questions. I ask them to raise their hand if they love to sing, dance, and draw. With each ascending class, fewer and fewer hands went up, and more and more eyes dimmed. I blamed it on our outdated manufacturing model for education. We don't need to be cogs in a wheel. We need to be free to fly! I'll get off my soapbox now since I have playmates here and I want to enjoy this moment to the fullest! And Scott, Bo is your man. He can write!"

Dec looks at his watch. "What a succinct group! Let's take a thirty-minute break. When we return, we'll talk about the common themes in our stories."

"I'm heading back to the house," says Auntie Pauline. "And I recommend drinking coconut water—*ono*. It's very good for the body."

John asks, "I know coconut water has many healing properties, but what is *ono*?"

"Delicious," answers Pauline as John, Pepper, and Rue move quickly to keep up with her.

"I'm going back that way, too," says Rachel. And the rest of the group goes with her. Payne moves beside Rachel, "I'm sorta *hopa*. I'm not half. I'm fractions, but I know firsthand what a tough road being different can be."

"Payne, I've learned that another word for being different is unique. You and I are unique," says Rachel. Payne smiles and tells Rachel he had arrived at the same conclusion.

Scott Green looks at the two of them. "Everyone is different, but the two of you had to face that issue sooner than homogeneous people."

"Rachel, Scott always takes a positive perspective," says Payne. Rachel nods and the three of them head toward the house.

When the group returns to the storytelling circle, Dec reminds them the same rules apply. Payne holds his jade turtle. "I heard many here speaking of the new principle as a children's sense of wonder and delight. I don't work with children; I work with adults. But if I see all of us as children of life like inner cells that make up the individual and individuals make up humanity, then is it our job to lead by example." Payne puts his jade turtle back.

Angelica holds a lava rock. "Everyone deserves an opportunity to explore in wonder and delight. I believe evolution comes through the journey of each life. If we can get this notion out into the world, we have a chance for a more joyful or cheerful world."

As Angelica puts down the lava rock, Eviann picks up the pink quartz and says, "My heart ached for what Dec just said about the lifeless eyes of children. I just want to cry whenever I think of it. The way I see it is that each of us has overcome an obstacle and has freed our intuitive self. Yes, we all lived an intuition-led life."

A number of heads nod in agreement. The sound of the water rushing up onto the sand can be heard, and a gentle breeze brushes against their hair and skin.

Scott holds the coconut. "Would we agree that we all listened to our own inner guidance system to get us here? Perhaps we should ask to know what should come next. For me, I think we need to get this message out to the larger community and the world. I think Rachel, Dec, Bo, or Payne could write up a collection of stories of adults who demonstrate, or model, as Angelica says, what can happen when we create a space for children to be."

Payne and Rachel gasp. Dec shouts, "No time." Scott puts the jade turtle down, and all heads and eyes go to Bo. Bo returns their looks with an enigmatic smile. With no object in hand, Rue speaks out, "Bo, could this story narrative project be your dream and bind you to a larger community?" Bo's eyes widen and his face lights up.

"Oh, what a wonderful idea!" shouts Angelica.

Auntie Pauline announces, "I think we are ready for the sacred ceremony. Tomorrow morning!"

"Bo and I asked for the connectivity of this group, of this retreat to be revealed. I think we just got our answer. I know we are all looking forward to the sacred ceremony tomorrow morning. Enjoy the rest of the day. Bo and I will be available if you want to talk with us about anything."

Auntie Pauline announces, "If you want to learn how to make some local kind of food, go to the kitchen. Dinner is at 6:30 P.M. Hawaiian time."

"That can mean anytime, but it will be somewhat close," says Rachel.

John approaches Auntie Pauline and asks about some local medicinal plants. Soon Auntie Pauline, Pepper, Rue, Angelica, and Pablo head out toward the sacred ceremony site.

"Wouldn't it be grand to cook some local food back home in Australia?" says Eviann to Donald.

"I think it would," replies William Edward, who faces Helena. The four of them head toward the kitchen.

Dec grabs Bo and stands in front of Scott Green and Payne Ow Porter. Dec says, "Tell me more about this book that you think Bo should write." Out of old habits, Bo shoots Dec a dirty look, and Scott and Payne laugh.

Scott says, "Do you have a sample of your work that I can see?"

"Sorry, I had a momentary relapse. I have free writing in my journal, and I have some technical reports," answers Bo.

"Bo and I met in college in a creative writing class," says Dec with a twinkle in his eye.

"You didn't mention that, Bo," kids Scott.

"Well, Dec has several published articles in magazines," says Bo.

Dec smiles and says, "I really don't have the time to devote to writing. Besides, Bo believes that our story is our legacy to life."

"Perhaps we need to wait and see what tomorrow's ceremony will bring," suggests Bo.

"A point well taken, and yet all we have is the moment," adds Scott.

Payne pats Bo on the back. "I feel for you, bro. Your friend Dec packs a wallop like my friend Scott. Perhaps it is best to go within and see if this project is yours or not."

"Sayers of truth are so maligned. Have you noticed that Dec?" asks Scott.

"I have. There is a wonderful parable about that, too. Basically, people avoid the naked truth, but truth dressed in story or parable clothes gets invited into many homes. Come on, Bo, clothe our stories and get us invited into many people's homes," shouts Dec.

"Remember, Bo, children speak the naked truth and get away with it all the time," says Scott. All four of them head toward the sand and toward the direction where the sun will eventually set.

For dinner, Auntie Pauline gathers the participants around a buffet table with all the food on it. She stands by a large serving bowl made of koa wood and she shares, "In Hawaii, this large serving bowl is known as calabash, where family and close friends share a meal. Come help yourself."

"The funny-looking sushi rolls were made by me," says Eviann.

"And me," shout Donald, Helena, and William.

"This is *huihui* chicken, Hawaiian barbecue," says Rachel. She proceeds to name each dish. "This is Japanese *namasu*, cucumber salad. This is *kumu* fish steamed Chinese style with black beans, ginger, and green onions. This is broiled short ribs in a Korean sauce of garlic, ginger, toasted sesame seeds, *shoyu* or soy sauce, sugar, and chopped green onions. And this is a regular garden salad. You have a choice of drinks: pineapple juice, guava juice, mango juice, coconut water, or water."

After dinner, the group takes their mini-beach chairs and sits close to the water. "Are we really meant to share our talent at the luau tomorrow night? This will be easy for Helena; what about the rest of us?" asks William.

"I'm too tired to sing," laments Helena.

"You have to stay up as long as you can," replies William.

"What time is it?" asks Helena.

"8:30 P.M.," says Donald Nelson. "Eviann and I can do 'Waltzing Matilda.'"

"Or I have been rather partial to '"Kookaburra Sits on the Old Gum Tree,' if you prefer," yawns Eviann.

"I could teach you all to sing 'Tiny Bubbles,'" says Rachel.

"Don't forget you are dancing with your sister," says Auntie Pauline.

"Maybe we could do a group singalong," says Angelica.

"Perhaps we should practice," says Pablo.

Auntie Pauline excuses herself to prepare for the morning ceremony. John and Pepper decide to retire, too, but Pepper announces, "I'll be doing tai chi on the beach early tomorrow morning, if anyone wants to join me."

So for thirty minutes the remaining group sings "Tiny Bubbles," "Michael Row the Boat Ashore," and "Lemon

Tree." At 9 P.M. the group dissipates. All are excited and want to be fully present for the sacred Hawaiian ceremony.

Early the next morning everyone except Auntie Pauline and Rachel are doing tai chi with Pepper as the sun comes over the horizon. No food is available; only the potent kava juice is served. Bo and Dec lead the group to the sacred site, where Auntie Pauline and Rachel are waiting for them.

Participants sit amphitheater style with Auntie Pauline standing in front of them and Rachel standing to the left side of Auntie Pauline, with a rock wall behind both of them. Once everyone is seated, she begins the call response. She chants and Rachel answers. With each set, the energy builds.

Helena looks above Auntie Pauline and puts her hands over her mouth. Her eyes tear up and she utters, "Great-Grandma Sasha! Grandma Nadya!"

"Great-Uncle Ambrose," cries Eviann.

"Is that him in the pink light?" asks Donald Nelson and Eviann nods in the affirmative. "Oh, I'm so thrilled to see him," whispers Donald to Eviann.

"Grandfather Laurence!" says William. John and Pepper smile and wave.

Payne stands up and bows to the larger-than-life spirit of the Chinese sage from his dream. Scott nudges his friend, "Wow, I'm impressed."

John and Pepper say to Angelica and Rue, "Li Wu, Ma Fun, and Dr. and Mrs. Chi Yu." Angelica and Rue stand up and give a slight bow. Dec laughs and pokes Bo. "Look, I see the two Williams—Shakespeare and William Wordsworth. They are my guides!"

"I'm not surprised," says Bo. "You talked about them enough."

Rachel notices the ancient ones and the Goddess Hauhet. Her thought returns to Egypt, and Rachel understands why sunlight never reaches the fourth statue, because primordial waters are incubation centers for things to come, for the right birthing moment.

Auntie Pauline notes the web of consciousness. Auntie Pauline speaks in a powerful, but trance-induced, voice, "The ancestors are here and they want to invite you to join the community of Lightbearers."

John Mee allows his guides to speak through him. "The Lightbearers are pleased you have come. We know many of you thought you came to see Angelica again, but you came for much more."

Pepper's guide speaks through her, "This community of Lightbearers is dedicated to keeping the sacred, natural child alive. The child of wonder and delight in each of you thrives."

Auntie Pauline's guides speak through her, "This community of Lightbearers lives in the moment and holds this truth, which you call the new principle, for the right moment to be released. We are attracted to your bright lights and wish to invite you to join us. We honor free will, so tell us with your voice or your mind if you want to complete this initiation."

Without hesitation, Angelica shouts, "I accept."

"Me, too," cries Eviann.

"Count me in," says Dec.

"Any group that wants me, I'm in," says Bo.

The rest of the group chooses to give a silent response of acceptance. After Scott Green gives his affirmative response, he smiles as he understands the guides would like to speak through him, and he consents. "When you come back to our world, we will not ask how many people you saved. We will ask how true you were to yourself. This seems like an easy task, but in fact is the most difficult. So share your lives and tell your stories."

Feeling the energy moving through her, Auntie Pauline's guides speak again, "The community of Lightbearers welcomes each one of you. We see you as our ground troopers working to free the natural gifts that come with children, but we want to remind you not to measure the progress of your work by earthly means. Remember, every life counts, so don't be discouraged. After all, life is eternal. Patience and a cheerful attitude make for joyful journeys and enchanting stories. Know we are always just a thought away. We send you our love and blessings. This initiation is complete." Auntie Pauline finishes speaking; the energy dissipates.

The group sits in total silence, soaking in the experience, marveling at what has just transpired. Finally, Scott Green says, "Whoa! That was so cool! I've never channeled a person before. That guide chose me! They know the power of print; so, Mr. Storyman," and he looks at Bo, "are you ready for this project?" Everyone laughs.

"I'm going to journal this. But do we truly believe the world is ready for this story?" asks Payne Porter.

Scott replies, "How can you ask such a question after what we've just experienced? Didn't you hear that we are already doing it! Don't ask, ground trooper. Just scatter the seeds!"

"History shows people are killed, like crucified, for speaking the truth," says Rachel, picking up on Payne's sentiments.

"This is true and so is the statement that truth will set you free. However, the growth process requires our hearts to break—break open—in order for that to happen," says Dr. Rue Mee, bringing balance back to the group.

"For sure. No real freedom until then," says Auntie Pauline.

Angelica cries out, "It is the Hundredth Monkey story. It's about one monkey living on a remote island off the coast of Japan. He discovers that sweet potatoes taste better when the grit is washed off. That monkey teaches other monkeys to do the same. When the hundredth monkey learns, monkeys everywhere know to do it. It doesn't take all of us, but we do need a critical mass. I don't care if I'm the first monkey or the last. I'm happy to be anywhere on that chain. What about the rest of you?"

Silence falls over the group. The initiation sinks in. This path is theirs and they have willingly chosen to accept and follow it. "I'm willing to let intuition lead," says Bo.

Dec stands up and comes down to the front to join Auntie Pauline. "I think it's time to celebrate our amazing initiation."

"Yes, and everyone can help," says Auntie Pauline.

"I hear there is a pig that has been cooking for some forty hours," says William. "Might we get a glimpse?"

"Sure can," says Rachel and motions William and whoever else is interested to follow her. Eviann, Donald, and Helena traipse along behind William and Rachel.

Dec asks Angelica, "Do you think this group needs to stay physically connected?"

"Marcum G. Garver has a wonderful online network. Since this is one of our grants, I suggest that we use email through the Marcum G. Garver server, especially since we have some international folks, as well as people across the country," answers Angelica.

"To stay connected with like-minded people sounds wonderful," says Payne.

Scott's eyes light up and he asks, "Angelica, can your organization fund a book project?"

"Yes! Oh, Scott, you are brilliant!" answers Angelica.

Dec pokes Bo. "Did you hear that?" Dec turns to Scott and asks, "What do you have in mind?"

Scott answers, "I think better when I'm moving. Let's go and walk on the beach." Payne excuses himself by saying, "I think I'm going to check on the pig."

The trade winds blow softly against the bodies of the three men. Finally, Scott answers, "Our goal is to use our stories as a living example of what is possible and to show how positive energy or this child of wonder and delight that lives within each of us can heal the earth and transform the consciousness of humankind, making people open to this new, I mean, old forgotten principle. We need the entire Mee family's stories. We need a mixture of age, culture, and gender, which would lend a nice universal appeal."

Bo marvels at Scott's ability to be so clear and concise. He thinks back on the stories he has heard and realizes how much he has learned through them. The men from Lewes touched him deeply. Maybe through doing this book project he can figure out what it is. His mother's cousins moved him. Eviann's rejection pushed him to look deeper inside himself. Dec is always propelling him forward, whether he wants to go or not. Dr. Rue Mee helped him to be free and to listen to his intuition. Yes, he needs to do this project, not just for the Community of

Lightbearers, but for himself. Then Bo laughs at the irony of it all. But of course, this is his dream!

Dec slaps Bo on the back and mentions, "You know Bo is a good researcher, too."

"That's good to know. So, Bo, what do you think?"

"I like what you've just said. I've started doing some research on Hawaiian and Swedish culture, since I was looking forward to meeting Auntie Pauline and Grandma Ashlar. Our group is rather large. Won't we have too much material?" asks Bo.

"I'm a good editor. How attached are you to what you write?" asks Scott back.

"Remember, I write for bids," replies Bo.

"Excellent, you can be concise. Just keep the message of a child's sense of wonder and delight in the forefront of your mind. So, Bo, are you the kind of person who needs a deadline?"

"I'm a good project manager," says Bo.

"Okay. We have the time now, so let's take a peek at your writing samples," suggests Scott and the three head back toward the house.

Bo, Dec, and Scott enter the kitchen to get to Auntie Pauline's office. They see Payne and Eviann chopping scallions and talking with Helena and William, who are dicing up tomatoes, with Rachel just listening.

Payne spots them and asks, "Scott, join us when you're done."

Bo hands Scott his project proposal and his journal. Scott skims the project proposal first and then opens to a page in the journal, and, finally, he smiles. "Dec, you're right. Bo can write." Scott addresses Bo. "You write with clarity and heart."

"Dec can write too. I'm not wiggling out of this project. But this project might need more than one person," says Bo.

"Bo, you make an excellent point. You will be the project director and can ask for help from anyone in the group. And, yes, that includes me." Scott heads toward Payne, Rachel, Helena, and William. Bo turns to Dec and says, "Dec, I think this is my dream."

Dec smiles back. "It must be. You're radiant and happy."

When the pig is lifted out of the pit wrapped in old *kappa* and mats, everyone gathers to watch the event. While the pig cools down, everyone goes into preparation mode. Inside the kitchen, *laulau* (fish wrapped in ti leaves), *lomi* salmon made with tomatoes and onions, and chicken long rice are being assembled and cooked. Pounded taro root, known as poi, is pulled out.

The feast is placed on the long tables decorated with anthurium, birds of paradise, and heliconia flowers. Rachel's sister, Leilani, places the *haupia* (coconut) and guava cakes in the calabash serving plate.

After the meal, Rachel, Auntie Pauline, Leilani, Malia (Rachel's mother), and the calabash kitchen helpers perform several hulas. Rachel leads the group in a popular Hawaiian song, "Tiny Bubbles." Donald Nelson and Eviann Adams teach the group the song "Waltzing Matilda."

Helena tilts her head toward Payne and Scott and says, "I've been asked to sing, 'The Wind beneath My Wings.' Feel free to join me." Only Helena's voice could be heard.

"Oh, Helena, that's so beautiful," cries Eviann.

"Helena, the way you sing captures spirit," says Rachel.

"If I knew you were taking requests, I would ask for 'Climb Every Mountain' or 'You Never Walk Alone' to remind us we are not alone in this journey of ours," says Angelica.

"No, we're not. There is a whole community of us!" shouts Dec.

"And I get to spend time with each of you," beams Bo. Eviann asks if the next group meeting could be in Sydney, Australia. Helena chimes in, recommending London, England, while Pablo, with mirth, says, "Or come home to the mother ship in Tempe, Arizona." Angelica comments that all these places are viable possibilities.

In an innocent voice, Bo suggests, "How about letting the child of wonder and delight decide?" Everyone laughs as they recognize the wisdom of his suggestion.

About the Author

Princess Cruises

Lorraine Lum Calbow holds a master's degree in counseling education, but her real training came from hours of listening to family and friends. Her love of people's stories, metaphors, and parables led her to reconnect with her own inner child of wonder and delight. She has published two nonfiction books, *This Light of Mine: Remembering the Light Within* and *Seeking the Light Within for the Directionally Impaired*. She has also written one children's picture book, *Smarly's Adventures* and has coauthored *The Art of Fine Whining or How Lori Lew Wrote Her Own Fortune Cookie* with Neil Weiner, PhD. *The Community of Lightbearers: Seven Stories of Reclaiming Wonder and Delight* is her first novel.